PRAISE FOR THE LARKIN DAY MYSTERY SERIES

"A smart, snarky series… Cozy mystery readers will adore Larkin Day."

BOOKLIFE, EDITOR'S PICK

"…an entertaining whodunit with a captivating amateur sleuth."

KIRKUS REVIEWS

"Ode to Murder is refreshing, and definitely recommended for fans of a good mystery. But it's also a great read for anyone who, like Larkin, is searching for a new story that can reach them in surprising, unexpected ways."

INDIEREADER

SHAKESPEARE IN THE PARK WITH MURDER

SHAKESPEARE IN THE PARK WITH MURDER

A LARKIN DAY MYSTERY

BOOK 3

NICOLE DIEKER

Cover design and interior design by Alan Lastufka.

First Edition published June 2023.

10 9 8 7 6 5 4 3 2 1

ISBN 978-1-959565-13-0 (Paperback)
ISBN 978-1-959565-14-7 (eBook)

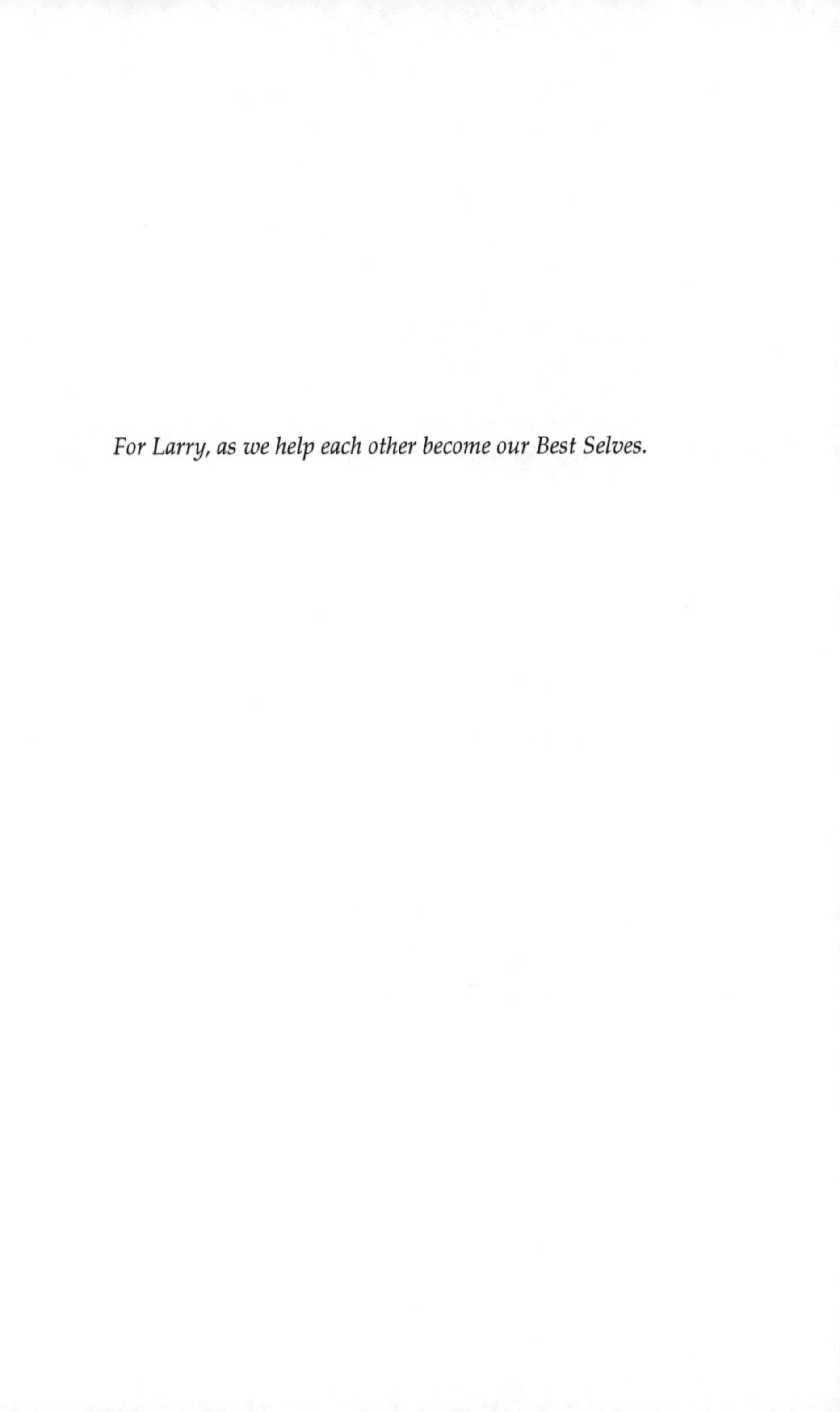

For Larry, as we help each other become our Best Selves.

DRAMATIS PERSONÆ

LARKIN DAY, an amateur detective, currently Interim Artistic Director of the Summer Shakespeare Festival

DR. JOSEPHINE DAY, her mother, formerly Dean of Students at Howell College

OFFICER CLAIRE NOVAK, her mother's girlfriend, currently a law enforcement professional

DR. ED JACKSON, her boyfriend, currently Assistant Professor of Music at Howell College and Musical Director of the Summer Shakespeare Festival

ANNI MORGAN, her best friend, currently a freelance writer with an emphasis in personal finance

ELLIOTT FOX, her best friend's boyfriend, formerly a professional magician with a short-lived television series

PAL, a golden retriever that lives with Larkin, Josephine, and Claire

THE SUMMER SHAKESPEARE FESTIVAL PRODUCTION TEAM

SAHIL MALHOTRA, Company Manager
BEATRIX YANG, Assistant Company Manager
VELVET BROWN, Stage Manager
CAMRYN KUNKEL, Assistant Stage Manager
PEG HAGGERTY, Lighting Designer
JIRO TAKASHI, Set Designer
STANLEY LEVINSTEIN, Costume Designer
ISABELLA WILLIS, Props Master
REBECCA BANKSHAW MORRIS, Assistant Props Master
PORTIA BREEDLOVE, Choreographer
SUSAN LEVINSTEIN, Dramaturg

SHAKESPEARE IN THE PARK WITH MURDER

CHAPTER 1

"It's hot," Larkin said, as she unzipped herself from her sleeping bag.

"I know," Ed said, setting down his free weights and helping Larkin free herself from the upper bunk. The cabins had bunkbeds, but no ladders; windows, but no air conditioning. The nearest outhouse was thirty feet away; the nearest facility that offered showers, flush toilets, and sinks was half a mile down the kind of packed-dirt runway that had been created, over the years, by people who needed to get to a functional bathroom as fast as they could. A *desire path*, Sahil had called it, when he gave Larkin and Ed the tour.

Larkin had not known, when she accepted the job of directing the newly relaunched Summer Shakespeare Festival, that it would involve camping. She knew, of course, that the performances would be outdoors, in a state-of-the-art amphitheater that boasted donor names on both its dressing rooms and many of its injection-molded seats. She had assumed that the rehearsals would be indoors. She had assumed that the meals would be served indoors, and that someone else would be responsible for cleaning the kitchen. She had assumed that she would be allowed to sleep in her own bed.

Technically, she could have. Sahil had seen her face when she first saw the cabins and had tactfully mentioned that one of the previous artistic directors had elected to drive home every evening. He had even more tactfully mentioned that this particular director had not been particularly well-liked among the company and had not lasted more than a single season.

"The kids want you to be a part of their experience," he explained.

Everyone called them *kids*, even though there was only one person in the company who wasn't a legal adult. Most of the kids were Howell College students. Some of them came from one of the other liberal arts colleges that mapped the boundaries of Eastern Iowa's Creative Corridor. There were a few grad students, a few retirees—"we call them *community members*," Sahil explained, "and they are essential to our mission"—and just enough Equity actors to allow the rest of them to earn Equity points.

The Equity actors got the cabin with the window air conditioner. They were also exempt from KP duty and latrine duty and all of the other uncomfortable duties, although nearly all of them pitched in. Everyone in the company understood that how they behaved today would affect the opportunities they received tomorrow. They were relentlessly, unnecessarily cheerful.

This suited Ed, who woke with the dawn to run four miles and rep his battered set of barbells. His black skin had darkened, under the Eastern Iowan sun. Larkin's white skin had turned red, and then white again, and she had spent part of one evening peeling it off in strips, and Sahil had driven up from Cedar Rapids the next day to bring her a bottle of sunscreen and an enormous floppy hat.

Sahil Malhotra—wealthy, well-connected, well-versed in both Shakespeare and the Festival—was their link to the outside world. He could have been a retiree, if he hadn't given himself the title of *company manager*. His assistant company manager, or ACM, stayed onsite. She slept in the same cabin as Larkin and Ed, although they rarely saw her. Beatrix Yang was the first one awake and the last one asleep, every day. That was her job—and it was why she was getting paid nearly as much as Larkin was.

Not that Larkin was at all dissatisfied with her compensation. Her nine-month contract paid well enough to allow her to satisfy both her creditors and her best friend Anni Morgan, who had responded to Larkin's offer first with congratulations and second with an offer of her own.

"Please let me help you create a financial plan," Anni had said, the two of them sitting side by side on Anni's sofa. "I could write about the process, if you wanted, for one of my freelance clients. Or we could just do it together because it would be fun!"

Larkin already knew that Anni's idea of *fun* was different from most people's. Comparing high-yield savings accounts, for example, was not what Larkin would consider *fun*—so she let Anni run the numbers on how much she could earn with an account with 3.00% APY that compounded on a monthly basis vs. an account with 2.75% APY that compounded daily, and picked the one that Anni picked for her. She also set up automatic monthly transfers from her checking to her savings account.

"It's called the *pay yourself first* method," Anni had said, "and it's the second-best way to save more money."

"What's the best way?" Larkin had asked.

"Earn more money, of course," Anni had said. "Which you have successfully done."

Larkin was not used to being successful. A year ago, she had been living in a Los Angeles apartment with seven roommates, working on a stalled dissertation while making minimum payments on maxed-out credit cards. Now she was sleeping in a four-person cabin with no air conditioning and no toilets, but she had already paid off one of her credit cards and had updated her resume to include the words *Artistic Director*.

She'd also updated her relationship status. Larkin Day and Ed Jackson were officially a couple. Sahil had made them sign a piece of paper, right after Larkin had signed her contract, stating that they would not allow their personal lives to affect their professional commitments to the Summer Shakespeare Festival.

"Sorry to put you through this," Sahil said, "but the Board insisted."

"Well," Ed said, signing his name under the words *Dr. Edward T. Jackson, Musical Director and Sound Designer*, "we all know what happened to the last guy."

He was referring to Manny Morris, the previous artistic director. Larkin had stepped into Manny's job after Manny had stepped out on his wife. His affair might not have affected the Festival, had he not selected the 21-year-old actress contracted to play Juliet—and so he was fired and she was encouraged to resign, and Larkin's first job had been to hire her replacement.

Which Larkin had successfully done. Farah Emerson had taken on the role of Juliet, and the former Juliet had sent Larkin a series of awkward, apologetic emails, and Larkin put a filter on her email to archive all messages from Amelia Jorgensen before they hit her inbox, and then she'd ended up at a place where they didn't even have email—out here, it was considered as unnecessary as toilet paper—and hadn't even thought about Manny or Amelia or any of their predecessors until Ed, helping Larkin down from the top bunk, brought them up.

"Manny's coming by this afternoon," he said. "Beatrix told me to tell you."

Larkin was about to ask how Beatrix could have gotten that information so quickly—she was pretty sure Beatrix had some kind of internet connection that the rest of them didn't have access to, and she was starting to feel a little envious of it—but their conversation was interrupted by a sleepy voice in the opposite bunk.

"Daddy's coming?"

This was Rebecca Morris, the 17-year-old assistant prop manager. Manny Morris was her father. He was also the reason she had been allowed into the company in the first place, daddy passing daughter an opportunity that could have been handled more professionally by someone else. Clarissa Bankshaw Morris, Rebecca's mother, was the reason she had been allowed to stay.

"We're not going to punish her for Manny's misdeeds," she had written, in a lengthy email that included a reference to lawyers. "It will be best, for everyone, if Rebecca remains an integral part of the Festival."

Larkin wasn't sure if it had been the right choice. Nobody had wanted Rebecca as their bunkmate, for starters—and so Rebecca had ended up in the same cabin as Larkin and Beatrix and Ed. This had disappointed Rebecca, who had hoped to make friends with the college students. It had also disappointed Larkin, who had hoped to spend some intimate time with Ed while Beatrix was off using her secret internet or whatever she did in the late evening and early morning hours. Rebecca Morris had yet to become an integral part of the Festival—she'd done very little to ingratiate herself, and most people found her grating—but she had already become an integral part of their lives.

"Yes," Larkin said, "your dad's coming."

"Good," Rebecca said, allowing a morning fart to break its way into the cabin. Ed opened the front door. Since Rebecca was the sole person in the company who was still underage, she had to remain supervised at all times; for the next hour, that responsibility would fall to Larkin.

"I'll see you at breakfast," Larkin told Ed. Then she picked Rebecca's towel off the floor and tossed it towards her. "Get your shower caddy," she said. "We've got forty-five minutes before the morning production meeting." There was no electricity in the cabins, and no place for anybody to charge their phones. Larkin's watch, which her mother had found in a shoebox, was nearly as old as Rebecca; a pair of white-gloved mouse hands kept the time.

"I hate camping," Rebecca said.

Larkin wanted to say *me too*—but she had to set a good example. "We're not camping," she said, picking up her backpack and plopping her floppy sunhat over her long, dark hair. "We're creating."

———

The first step in the creation process was, of course, the morning production meeting—and the first person to present, after everyone had settled around the table with their plates of pancakes and granola and bacon and eggs, was the lighting designer.

"Everything's ready for Hang and Focus on Saturday," Peg said. "The crew will be here at 10 a.m.."

Peg was the oldest member of the production team. She was the only member of the team who had been born in Iowa; the only member who had been participating in Summer Shakespeare since it was an all-volunteer event. There were old photos of a young Peg, long-haired and fairy-winged, helping to place the ass head on Bottom in *A Midsummer Night's Dream*. She'd designed lights for that show, too. Back then, everyone had done everything. Now, Peg and Beatrix needed to coordinate a team of union electricians to hang and focus an array of lights that were so high-tech—and so expensive—they required their own corporate sponsor.

Peg, who was now short-haired and tool-belted, had also briefly dated Larkin's mother's girlfriend. "Claire and I were together for about a year," she had explained. "No hard feelings on either side. Glad she's happy."

Peg was the kind of person who wanted everybody to be happy—and meant it. She had learned, somewhere between her first and her twentieth Summer Shakespeare, how to function in a way that allowed her to help other people without diminishing her own resources. She tied a red bandana around her buzz cut to keep the sweat from getting into her eyes; underneath, she glowed.

Rebecca, shunned by the majority of the company, took shelter next to Peg. This meant that Isabella, the graduate student who was serving as props master, had to sit on the other side of Rebecca. It also meant that Isabella was next to speak; she had very little to say, and none of it included the high school student who was supposed to spend the summer assisting with props. Most of Isabella's production was directed not towards Larkin, the artistic director who was ostensibly leading the meeting—even though Beatrix, the assistant company manager, was the one managing all of the components that made it run smoothly —but towards Jiro.

Jiro Takashi was the set designer. He had the most impressive resume of anyone at the table. He also had the most impressive compensation package, although Larkin was one of the few people who knew that. After Jiro had been added to their production team, there had been articles not only in the *Cedar Rapids Gazette* and the *Iowa City Press-Citizen*, but also *Playbill* and the arts section of *The New York Times*.

Isabella was smitten. Jiro was not—but Larkin suspected that Isabella and Jiro had slept together the previous night. They hadn't signed a contract, the way she and Ed had. They'd never have what Jiro would call a relationship. Isabella would call it a relationship after the fact, because she'd need something to make herself feel better about what hadn't happened.

Next to Jiro were Susan-and-Stanley. Dramaturgy and costumes, respectively, although much of their work overlapped. Susan-and-Stanley had signed their contract, although they hadn't needed to; SuStan, as they were inevitably known, had been married for longer than Larkin had been alive. They had worked their way through a few of the major Shakespeare festivals and several of the minor ones before settling themselves in the relative affordability of Eastern Iowa. Susan's accent was softly British; Stanley's was loudly Brooklyn. They were well-liked but standoffish; they always seemed to be putting on a dog-and-pony show. Susan, with her mane of graying hair, was the pony. Stanley, affable and barking with laughter, was the dog.

Velvet, the stage manager, sat on the other side of Stanley. Camryn, the assistant stage manager, sat on the other side of Velvet. These two had also worked together in the past, passing messages back and forth over headsets—but it was their first Summer Shakespeare, and their first time doing any kind of professional theater. Velvet had been recruited from the Creative Corridor community theater circuit, and her compensation package had been adjusted accordingly. Camryn, who had turned 18 two weeks before rehearsals started, wasn't getting paid at all.

Beatrix was next to Camryn; Larkin was next to Beatrix. Then Ed, of course. The last seat at the round table—the one between Ed and Peg—belonged to Portia.

Portia Breedlove was the choreographer. A ringer, like Jiro Takashi. A hoofer, with credits that had taken her from New York to Los Angeles and back again. She'd danced in the background of two Hollywood musicals. She'd landed small roles—scientist, servant, sex worker—on a few popular streaming series. She had very nearly made it into *The Lion King*.

Portia was everything Larkin was not: poised, cultured, beautiful, well-turned-out. Portia was also Black, which meant that she and Ed were able to have certain kinds of conversations that Larkin was by default excluded from. Some of those conversations were in French, which Portia had learned from her mother and Ed had learned from books. Not that Larkin included Ed in all of her conversations—last night, for example, she'd had a tête-à-tête with Rebecca about how often to wash her hair—but whenever she saw Ed and Portia together, she saw the contract they hadn't needed to sign. *Black folk stick together*, as Ed had put it.

So Larkin stuck to the business at hand, and when Ed squeezed her hand before carrying off her plate—it was his day to help with the dishes—she trusted that it still mattered. Theater was all about trust, after all. So was falling in love.

Larkin had written Anni about all of this, belly-down on her upper bunk, using a flashlight to illuminate her haphazard handwriting. Anni had written back, composing the letter at her laptop before printing it out and putting it in the mail.

> *The best thing that can happen this summer is for you to be your best self.*
>
> *If you are the best version of Larkin, then the Festival will have the best version of* Romeo and Juliet. *Other versions may be acceptable, of course, but you have the opportunity to create the best one—so don't get distracted by anything that isn't directly related to your goal.*

Anni's letters often included the word "goal." They also included frequent mentions of Elliott Fox, the great love of Anni's life. The two of them had recently become reunited, after a series of circumstances contrived to keep them apart, and they were in the process of buying a home.

> *I don't know what the best version of Larkin looks like,* Anni's letter continued. *I'm not sure we've seen her yet. I'm still figuring out how to be the best version of Anni. Sometimes I tell Elliott that I am astounded that he was able to love all of the previous versions of me, before their successive upgrades. He tells me that he could see my code compiling.*

Elliott was a freelance programmer, specializing in some kind of software development that Larkin didn't fully understand. Before that, he had been a professional magician, specializing in card tricks and sleight-of-hand. He could pick locks and open back doors. Larkin didn't know why Anni had picked him—Elliott was a classic nerd, the kind of man who knew everything about Python and believed that any shirt with buttons qualified as formalwear—but she knew that Anni was happy.

I'm not qualified to make programming metaphors, so I'll make a personal finance one instead, Anni's letter had finished. *It's the pay-yourself-first method, again. Be the best Larkin and everything else will follow. Don't give Ed the chance to fall in love with Portia because you're indebted by distractions, including the distraction of whether Ed will fall in love with Portia. Give yourself what you need to be the best Larkin you can be, and give Ed the chance to fall in love with the person you become. If he doesn't, at least you won't spend the rest of your life thinking "he would have loved me if I hadn't been so [insecure][overworked][cranky][etc.]"*

You'll probably want to write me back and say, "I don't know how to be the best Larkin I can be," so don't waste the stamp. Instead, start looking around you and asking yourself what is worth paying attention to. You're good at that. It's how you solve your mysteries.

Larkin, sitting at the production table, looked around her and asked herself what was worth paying attention to. Isabella and Jiro's non-relationship drama would work itself out on its own, and if it were necessary for anyone to mediate, it would be Sahil. SuStan wouldn't cause any trouble, though Larkin doubted she'd know them any better at the end of the summer than she did right now. Velvet and Camryn were still thrilled to be here, despite the fact that they were only hired to balance the budget, and the two of them were currently negotiating the intricacies of Tech Week with Beatrix and Peg. Ed was on Kitchen Patrol. Portia was sipping coffee—and for a minute Larkin was jealous of the way Portia drank her coffee, every delicate movement a combination of ballet, modern, and jazz —and Rebecca was staring at her coagulating eggs.

"Hey," Larkin said, to the one person who demanded attention without being worth it. "Did you and Isabella end up finding a pair of daggers you liked?"

Romeo and Juliet both wore daggers, although Juliet's was easier to overlook; she carries it with her whenever she leaves the home, places it next to her before she drinks the sleeping potion, and leaves it behind when she is carried to the tomb. Nearly everyone wore daggers in Shakespeare's day, Susan had explained. "They were versatile multitools, rather like our smartphones." Isabella had decided that the lovers' daggers, like their houses, should be alike in dignity. "Like, you know, the way people bond over liking the same brands. Maybe the pommel should be an apple."

Larkin had encouraged Isabella to come up with a better solution. Now she encouraged Rebecca to explain it.

"We found one and we made one," Rebecca said. "Juliet's dagger is an antique. We got it in Iowa City. Romeo's is a prop dagger with the blade that goes up into the handle, since he has to stab himself with it."

"Juliet stabs herself," Larkin gently corrected, "with Romeo's dagger." She and the actors had been spending most of their time on scene work, so Rebecca—who wasn't even present at most of the rehearsals—couldn't necessarily be blamed for not knowing the show in full.

"I thought Juliet took the poison."

"Juliet takes the sleeping potion," Larkin explained. She had gone over this many, many times back when she taught Theater 101. "Friar Laurence, who married Romeo and Juliet in secret, gave Juliet the potion so she could pretend to be dead so she wouldn't have to marry Paris."

"Why didn't she just tell her parents she was already married?"

"Because Romeo had just killed her cousin Tybalt," Larkin said, "and had been banished."

"Ban-ish-*ed*," Rebecca said, correcting her director.

"Right." Larkin said, smiling. "So Romeo believes Juliet is really dead. He was supposed to get a letter explaining the whole thing, but the person who was supposed to deliver the letter got quarantined due to plague." This part of the play was very easy to miss, although Larkin was determined to ensure her audience understood it. "Romeo buys some poison from an apothecary and heads over to Juliet's tomb so that he can kill himself next to her body. Paris tries to stop him, so Romeo kills Paris." Larkin pulled in closer to Rebecca, as if to whisper a secret. "Romeo wasn't exactly being his best self at the moment."

"He was being a murderer," Rebecca whispered back.

"Right," Larkin said again. She hadn't really thought of Romeo as a murderer before. If she was going to be both a professional theater director and an amateur detective, she should start thinking more carefully about these things. "Anyway, Romeo takes the poison and dies. Juliet wakes up, sees that Romeo is dead, decides she no longer wants to live, tries to drink from the empty poison bottle, and then stabs herself with Romeo's dagger."

"Pile of corpses, the end," Rebecca said. One of the actors had said that, at the first rehearsal. Everyone else had stopped saying it two weeks ago—so Larkin ended the conversation the way Shakespeare had. "For never was a story of more woe," she said, standing up and adjusting her floppy sunhat. "Than this of Juliet and her—"

But Larkin's couplet was interrupted by another voice.

"I am going to *kill you*."

CHAPTER 2

Larkin had never met Clarissa Bankshaw Morris. She knew, of course, that Clarissa was a member of the Bankshaw family, and that she was either directly or distantly related to the enormous brokerage that F. H. Bankshaw, Sr. had originated—and the enormously popular roboadvisor app that Freddie Bankshaw, Jr. had launched the previous year—but the Bankshaw investment firm hadn't been on Anni's shortlist of places for Larkin to put her money, and so Larkin hadn't thought about it since. She hadn't even looked Clarissa Bankshaw Morris up online; Larkin had been hired as a director, not a detective, and it felt inappropriate to investigate. But Larkin knew, just by looking, that this woman was Rebecca's mother. It was also obvious that this woman was Manny Morris's wife—the monogrammed bag, the diaphanous scarf, the giant diamond on her left hand—and that she was, somewhat tragically, attempting to hurt her husband by threatening to hurt her child.

Rebecca knew this, too. "Daddy isn't here," she said.

"I don't care," Clarissa said, even though she clearly

did. Her head kept twisting, one direction and then another, not wanting to miss Manny's arrival. "Look at you," she said, as she looked over her left shoulder. "You haven't brushed your hair. You aren't using that facial scrub I bought you. Your T-shirt looks like it spent the night on the floor."

"It's camping," Rebecca said. "We don't have, like, chests of drawers."

"Those young people look like they've figured out how to dress themselves," Clarissa continued, gesturing towards the cluster of actors who were doing Alexander exercises with Portia. "Why aren't you over there with them? Making friends? Connecting with people? I did not defend your right to participate in this festival so you could sit by yourself and get to know the kitchen staff."

That's when Larkin realized that Clarissa Bankshaw Morris had never met *her*. She stood up, giving Manny Morris's wife the full view. Tall, with wide hips and sunburned shoulders, wearing a floppy hat, a pair of extra-large shorts, a triple-strength sports bra, and a tank top that had spent the night hanging off the corner of her bunk. "I'm Larkin Day," she said, holding out her hand and hoping it was still slightly greasy from breakfast. "Artistic director."

"Oh," Clarissa said. Larkin watched Clarissa size her up. She was used to this. Everyone took a few seconds to take Larkin in, and most of them raised first their eyes —*yes*, Larkin wanted to tell them, *I get my height from my deadbeat dad*—and then their eyebrows. "I'm sorry," Clarissa said, accepting Larkin's handshake with a dismissive up-and-down grasp, "we hadn't been properly introduced."

Then she turned back to Rebecca. "You should have let

me know that you were spending time with the artistic director. I would have loved to know more about her."

The implication, of course, was that Rebecca should have been spying on Larkin—and the fact that Rebecca hadn't made Larkin re-evaluate her bunkmate. She gave Rebecca's shoulder an approving squeeze and watched Rebecca's mother flinch.

"Ask me anything you want," Larkin said. "I'd be happy to discuss the production with you. We're two days out from Tech Week, but I'm sure you already knew that."

Clarissa had already known that. Tech Week was the most stressful part of the rehearsal process, although much of the stress could be mitigated with adequate preparation —and Larkin wondered if Manny and Clarissa had timed their visits to prevent Larkin from having time to do her work.

"We don't need to talk shop," Clarissa said, "although I'm always interested in how female directors manage to get it all done." She glanced at Larkin's hands. "I suppose you don't have a husband? Children?"

"I'd be happy to discuss my personal life," Larkin said, "if that's what you're after."

"She solved a murder," Rebecca said, pulling out the most interesting part of Larkin's personal life and aiming it at her mother's midsection. "Before she got hired to do Summer Shakespeare."

"Two murders, actually," Larkin said. The second murder hadn't exactly involved a dead body, but there were ways of killing people that didn't involve corpses— as Clarissa Bankshaw Morris clearly understood.

"How interesting," she said, in a way that would have diminished everything Larkin had ever done if Larkin had not already committed to becoming her Best Self. "I heard you were a last-minute hire. Interim, just for the season."

Larkin stood tall, and did not let Clarissa tear her down. "The Board will be conducting a national search for a permanent artistic director next fall, but—"

"But Sahil had Larkin on his shortlist for nearly a year." Ed, coming out of the camp kitchen, had caught the end of the conversation. "He was just waiting for the right opportunity."

"Dr. Jackson," Clarissa said. Larkin had noticed that white people liked to refer to Ed by his academic title. Some people did it to prove they weren't racist. Clarissa did it to put Ed in his place.

"They're dating," Rebecca said. "Larkin and Ed."

"Nearly a year," Ed said again. He was stretching the word *nearly* to its sticking point, but it didn't matter. Larkin watched Clarissa register this information, adding it to the ledger she was keeping in her mind. Clarissa needed to convince herself that she was better than Larkin, and she needed to communicate her conviction. She was trapped—and so the best version of Larkin, the one she would tell Ed about later that day and write Anni about later that night, decided to set her free.

"We're about to start rehearsal," Larkin said. "Would you like to sit with me?"

———

"I cannot believe you did that," Ed said. He had been saying that a lot, that summer. He always smiled when he said it, which seemed like a good sign. "You let Clarissa Bankshaw Morris sit next to you all morning long. You asked her what she thought. You incorporated one of her ideas."

"It was something I was going to do anyway," Larkin said. "I didn't incorporate any of her bad ideas." She took a sip of her coffee. The Coffee Shop, which had been Larkin's former employer before she had been hired as Artistic Director—the barista-to-director path being fairly standard in the theater world—was Summer Shakespeare's exclusive coffee-and-tea supplier. Larkin had set up the meeting, Sahil had done the negotiation, and once a week Beatrix drove to Pratincola to pick up fresh supplies.

"But still," Ed said. "She left happy."

"That was the whole point," Larkin said. "Haven't you ever had, like, the misbehaving student who just wants a few minutes of your undivided attention?"

"I think everyone here wants a few minutes of your undivided attention," Ed said. He tilted his head towards Larkin and kissed her. "Which means that right now, everyone here is just a little bit jealous of me."

Larkin and Ed had gotten into the habit of *going-on-a-date,* as Ed had originally phrased it, during the hour-long break between the company lunch and the afternoon rehearsal. Larkin could have used that time to hold meetings or coach actors. Sahil had suggested—and Beatrix had insisted—that Larkin use that time to rest.

So she and Ed sat together, as they did every afternoon, on a blue-painted bench in front of a body of water that was not quite large enough to be called a lake. This bit of Eastern Iowa was not technically part of the campground. Beatrix had said they could sit there anyway.

"How is your mother doing?" Ed asked. Larkin had gotten a letter from her mother in that day's mail. "I don't know," Larkin said, reaching into the backpack that she used to carry her script, legal pad, water bottle, and other necessities. "Let's find out."

She opened the letter and read aloud:

I hope this letter finds my daughter well
  As I myself can also claim to be;
  Perhaps she'll guess the news I have to tell—
  I've started teaching people poetry.

Josephine Day had been the Dean of Howell College for just over a decade. Before becoming an academic administrator, she had taught poetry, rhetoric, and composition at a handful of colleges and universities. She was now either retired or between careers, depending on what day it was —and which Day she felt like being at the moment.

The classes meet on Wednesdays every week
  The library has set aside a room
  And students of all ages come to seek
  Instruction in both structure and in mood.

Larkin's mother had included an aside—*sorry for the slant rhyme*—before concluding:

One should not ask if I am getting paid
  We both know I can live on what I've earned
  With time to give to others what I've made
  And share with other people what I've learned.
  The best surprise of course turns out to be
  I learn as much from them as they from me.

"She sent me a Shakespearean sonnet," Larkin said. Then she pulled out the other piece of paper that had been placed inside the envelope. "Claire sent a note, too. Literally."

Larkin's mother's girlfriend, the compact and practical Officer Claire Novak, had written her message on a sticky note.

We're sure you're doing great
  Your mom's doing great too
  The dog not so much
  Say hi to Peg

"I guess that one's blank verse," Ed quipped.

"Doggerel," Larkin quipped back—although she was worried, just a little bit, about Claire's aging golden retriever. Not about the dog itself; Pal had lived a very long and very happy life, full of head scritches and ride-alongs. The good brand of kibble. Bits of people food, passed underneath kitchen tables—and that was what Larkin was worried about. What Claire would do with her hands, in the evenings, when she could no longer use them to care for her dog. Larkin's mother was not the cuddly type; when Larkin was growing up, the two of them twitched their noses at each other, *Bewitched*-style, instead of giving hugs. Claire would need something to pet and play with. To circle the block with, twice a day.

They'd need to get a puppy, probably—or Larkin would need to have a baby.

"I'll write them back later this evening," Larkin said, standing up. She would not think about puppies or babies or what that meant for her-and-Ed or whether she even wanted a puppy, barking and making messes and tearing up the house that she and her mother shared with Claire. *Do not let yourself become indebted by distractions*, Anni had written—and so Larkin, taking one more action that Ed would have found unbelievable if she had been able to tell him about it, *did not*.

Instead, she and Ed walked back to the campground—where they found the entire company gathered in a cluster, attracted by the arrival of Manny Morris.

Ed sang softly, setting the tenor of the situation: "Oh

come, oh come, Emmanuel." His joke, meant just for Larkin's ears, was apt; Manny Morris had acted the role of Jesus Christ multiple times, in both its Superstar and traditional versions. He'd been cast as Romeo nearly as often; Rebecca had shown Larkin photos of her father in various stages of the play. Now Manny was playing Santa Claus, distributing gifts indiscriminately to actors and crew.

"Who wants some energy bars?" he asked, reaching into his satchel. "I know you're about to begin Tech Week. Susan, you remember—*The Tempest*, five years ago?"

"I do," Susan said. "You wanted to use real water. Like Mary Zimmerman's *Metamorphoses*."

"And we did," Manny said. "Peg, you remember?"

Peg did. "We spent every night cleaning up wet sand," she said, in a way that was just assertive enough to imply her reservations. She was one of the few company members who did not accept any of the gifts that Manny had stuffed into his bag.

"Mimi," Manny said. "Make sure some of these get to the kids in the back."

A young woman moved among the company, passing out what appeared to be foil-wrapped condoms—and Larkin was less shocked by the fact that Manny Morris was handing out prophylactics than she was by the woman he had conned into his former domain.

The impenetrable Amelia Jorgensen.

Larkin would never have cast Amelia as Juliet, though she understood why Manny had. The twenty-one-year-old Amelia could have passed for a fourteen-year-old girl, easily. But her irresistibility was false, unless you were a middle-aged man who needed someone who would only feint towards resistance. Amelia, fresh out of Waterloo, was a bottom-feeder who had just grown legs. She'd attached herself to Manny, letting her tendrils of hair settle onto his shoulder. They'd both told themselves they were evolving.

Farah Emerson, on the other hand—and Larkin watched Amelia reach her hand out to Farah before pulling it away—was the real thing. Farah was nearly thirty, with a decade of professional credits. She didn't need to pass for a teenage girl; she inhabited Juliet so fully that the seams flattened. There was no hook on which disbelief could be suspended; no mark that indicated what was missing.

Farah was also dark-skinned, with hair that reflected blue and gold, and although Larkin had thought about reflecting Romeo's *it is the East* in Juliet's costuming and background, she had left it alone. Juliet would not stand in for cultural commentary, not in this production. She was not a metaphor; she was a necessity. Juliet, as played by Farah Emerson, was *the sun*—and so Amelia orbited around her and settled next to her former scene partner.

Tyler Mackintosh was another one of Manny's picks, and although he had originally been cast as Romeo to offset Amelia's lack of craft, he had reset himself towards Farah's standard. A fair-headed, flexible actor-combatant, Tyler was malleable enough to fit in anywhere. Romeo was Everyman, after all. Fortune's fool, shaping himself to his surroundings until he ends up in a tomb.

Romeo was also a murderer, as Rebecca had reminded her earlier that morning.

Larkin, watching Tyler make polite conversation with Amelia, wondered if there was time to adjust her production to highlight this facet of Romeo's personality. They were about to start Tech Week, which meant that she couldn't do much with staging or lights or sets or costumes, not if she didn't want to become known as one of those directors who changes everything at the last minute and gives everybody a bunch of extra work.

Maybe Romeo would have to be one of those murderers that nobody suspected, right until the moment when he started killing people. That was how it usually happened, anyway. If someone went around acting like they had the capacity to murder—well, then they'd be like Clarissa Bankshaw Morris.

"Do you know where Clarissa went?" Larkin asked Ed. If Manny's soon-to-be-ex-wife had wanted to confront her soon-to-be-former-husband, she was missing her opportunity.

"No," Ed said. "Maybe she's with Rebecca."

Larkin tried to see if Manny and Clarissa's daughter was in the crowd. "Do you see her?"

"Or maybe Clarissa is just a poor player," Ed continued, "that struts and frets her hour upon the stage—"

He looked to Larkin to complete the line—they often finished each other's sentences—but Larkin, who was still looking for Clarissa and Rebecca, missed her cue.

"*And then is heard no more*," Ed said. "Come on, Larkin, I know you know your *Macbeth*."

"Ed!" Larkin said. "I know *you* know that you are never, *ever* supposed to say the name of the Scottish Play aloud!"

"You do not seriously believe that I just cursed your production," Ed said. "The whole *Macbeth* thing is just a tale full of sound and fury, signifying nothing."

"Ed," Larkin said again. "Stop."

"Fine," Ed said, and Larkin looked around her company, distracted by its pair of interlopers, and hoped that Ed had not just sentenced two of its members to die.

CHAPTER 3

Three days later, Larkin wrote Anni a letter. Like most of her summer correspondences, it was scribbled on the same yellow legal pad she used to take notes during rehearsals.

Dear Anni,

Best Self Larkin is having her best Tech Week ever. People keep telling me how surprised they are that everything's going well. Ed says it's because there's no drama, and then of course he said, "pun intended."

I think it's because I'm trying very, very hard to not get distracted by anything. It's not easy. Manny and Amelia keep showing up. I asked Beatrix if she could just ban them from the campground or something like that, but she said that Summer Shakespeare made a rule long ago that all of its rehearsals would be open to the public. I asked Peg about it, and she said that they made the rule when Summer Shakespeare was so small that it rehearsed in a public park. She thinks they should change the rule. I'll ask Sahil about that after the season is over.

Until then I'll just have to play nice with the former Artistic Director and his former Juliet.

"Pun intended," Ed said, when I told him.

If that's the curse Ed brought onto the production by saying the M-word aloud, twice—the curse of Manny and Amelia, not the curse of puns—I can deal with it! Not that I believe in curses, or at least I wouldn't if we were back in Pratincola. But theater makes you rethink what you believe. That's kinda the whole point.

Write back and tell me how the house-hunting is going. I know nothing about buying a house and I am sure you know everything. You can even give me all of the boring details about comparing mortgages, if you want!

Larkin

P.S. Since all of the rehearsals are open to the public, you and Elliott should come to the first dress rehearsal on Monday. 6 p.m. I'd like to get an outsider's perspective before I make any final tweaks. You can pretend I didn't just call you an outsider.

The response came not from Anni, but from Beatrix.

"Your friends Anni and Elliott are coming to the dress rehearsal," the assistant company manager said, glancing at her phone and reading what appeared to be an email. Larkin still didn't know how Beatrix got email. She wondered if Beatrix drove offsite every morning, to find a spot with cell service and download the day's news. She wondered if she could slip Beatrix a twenty dollar bill to look up the latest celebrity gossip.

"Your parents are also coming," Beatrix continued. "Your friend Anni said she invited them."

Larkin was momentarily confused. Her father, whom she had not seen since she was three years old, could not possibly—"Oh, you mean Mom and Claire."

"Yes," Beatrix said, reading the email aloud. "Please tell Larkin that we invited Josephine and Claire. They had us over for dinner last night and spent the entire time asking how Larkin was doing, so Elliott and I thought they should find out for themselves. I hope they won't be a distraction."

Adding Larkin's mother to the mix might have been a distraction at the beginning of the summer—but Larkin's Best Self, the person she had been rehearsing for the past four weeks, was ready.

"Tell them they're all welcome," she said, "and thank you."

Beatrix nodded and moved on to the next item on her to-do list. Larkin looked at the next item on hers—a meeting with Isabella to discuss swapping Juliet's sleeping potion for something in a slightly bigger bottle—and made her way towards the props shed. When she got there, she found Rebecca sitting guard.

"You can't go in there," Rebecca said, gesturing towards the shed with one dispirited shoulder.

"Why not?"

"Because Isabella and Jiro are in there," Rebecca said. "They're supposed to be done by now."

"And you're supposed to be supervised," Larkin said. "At all times."

"I'm supervising myself," Rebecca said. "Isabella said it was okay."

"I don't think Beatrix Yang or Sahil Malhotra would say it was okay," Larkin said. She chose her words carefully, deliberately eliminating her own opinion on the matter. "And I'm sure your parents wouldn't want to know that you'd been left alone."

"I wish I was a fourteen-year-old girl in Fair Verona," Rebecca said, "instead of a seventeen-year-old girl in Unfair Iowa."

"No, you don't," Larkin said, sitting down next to Rebecca. "Juliet's parents basically owned her. She was an asset they could barter for status." It occurred to Larkin that Rebecca's situation was somewhat similar. She hoped it wouldn't occur to Rebecca. "Who you really want to be is Romeo. He had all the freedom."

"But Romeo isn't as smart as Juliet," Rebecca said. "He's impulsive. He murders a bunch of people."

"Just two people," Larkin said, "and they'd probably count as voluntary manslaughters. That's when you kill someone on purpose, but you don't plan it in advance. Heat-of-passion kind of thing." She'd researched the different types of homicide, back when she was considering becoming a private detective instead of a professional director. Sitting next to Rebecca, watching her smile, Larkin knew she'd made the right choice.

"And the Capulets and the Montagues still decide to make a solid gold statue of Romeo's body," Rebecca said. "Next to Juliet's. Because he sacrificed himself to their enmity."

"Glad to know someone's paying attention," Larkin said—and then the door opened, smacking Rebecca in the back and pitching her forward into the dirt.

"Sorry," Isabella said to Larkin.

"We didn't know you'd be there," Jiro said to Rebecca.

Larkin could see the words swell Rebecca's throat—*you told me to be there*—and then she saw Rebecca swallow them down. Larkin wondered if Rebecca had a crush on Jiro as well. He was handsome enough, although his credits were the real attraction. When Larkin had been a graduate student, she would have wanted to spend as much time with a working professional like Jiro Takashi as possible, even if it meant behaving unprofessionally.

But Isabella was the graduate student, and Larkin was

the artistic director, and so after they'd completed their meeting and found an appropriate swap for the potion bottle, Larkin pulled Isabella aside—keeping Rebecca within eyeshot, though not earshot—and said, "You're not supposed to leave Rebecca unsupervised. She's seventeen. You remember how it was, when you were her age."

Isabella was a young graduate student, not yet twenty-three, which meant that she had grown up with a level of adult supervision that Larkin, who had turned thirty-six in April, had largely missed. When Larkin had been a little girl, her mom had let her wait in the car while she ran errands. By the time Isabella was growing up, that simple introduction to responsibility had turned into child endangerment. For kids Rebecca's age, it was even worse—one of the first things Rebecca had said, upon discovering that their campground had neither Wi-Fi nor cell service, was "does that mean my mom won't know where I am?" Clarissa Bankshaw Morris had installed an app on Rebecca's phone, giving her the ability to monitor her child's location at all times. Rebecca couldn't even trick the app by leaving her phone in a backpack or a school locker; her phone held a record of her habitual movements, and any atypical inactivity triggered an alarm.

But on camp, Rebecca was free—and so was Isabella. Larkin saw, in the young woman's face, what a lifetime of surveillance had created. Smartphones, smartwatches, computer-chipped campus IDs; Isabella had worn devices without developing them. She hadn't learned the kind of self-management that came from five minutes in a parking lot, an afternoon in an empty apartment, the opportunity to walk to and from the bus stop alone. Like Romeo, she had become fortune's fool—commanded and commended by apps and brands, her wearables monitoring her where-abouts and sharing her data with the parent companies involved—and like Juliet, she had thrown herself at the first man who promised any kind of escape.

"If it happens again, I'll have to inform Sahil," Larkin said—knowing, as she said it, that it was an empty threat. Isabella had already deposited her paycheck. The programs had already been printed. Even if they asked her to leave, three days before Preview Night, Isabella would have sufficient proof that she had done the work. It wouldn't hurt her resume. It would only hurt Larkin, the Artistic Director who prevented two young people from carrying out their doomed summer-camp romance. They'd find a way to re-hire Manny Morris, and Larkin would go back to being a barista.

―――

"Going back to The Coffee Shop," Larkin told Ed, during their date, "would be the worst outcome."

"I don't know," Ed said, breaking off a piece of his chocolate chip cookie and passing it to Larkin. "I can think of worse ones."

Larkin accepted the chunk of cookie. Then she broke it in half and passed the larger piece back to Ed. "Like what?"

"Well," Ed said, "The Coffee Shop could burn down. So you wouldn't even get to be a barista. You'd have to find another job."

"Would the entire apartment building burn down," Larkin asked, "or just The Coffee Shop?"

"It would be a very localized fire," Ed said. "Anni's apartment would be safe."

"Not like she's going to be living there for much longer," Larkin said, worrying her bit of Ed's cookie between her fingers. "She's going to end up buying a house right after we get done with the Festival, and we're going to end up helping her move. And she won't even order us pizza afterwards, because Anni doesn't order pizza. She'll make it herself, and it'll be a whole-wheat crust with broccoli on top, and then she'll put something weird in like figs."

"Broccoli-fig pizza," Ed said. "It actually doesn't sound that bad."

"And then Manny will get re-hired as the Summer Shakespeare director, or they'll find someone else, and I'll have to go back to being a barista, and then The Coffee Shop will burn down." Larkin smooshed her cookie crumbles together and transferred them to her mouth. "But it will be a very localized fire, and nobody will get hurt, so that's a plus."

"And that kind of localized, no-casualty fire has insurance-claim arson written all over it," Ed said, "which means that it would be a mystery for you to solve."

"But I'd still have to find another job," Larkin said, wiping her chocolate-stained fingers on her pants. "And that could take time away from my mystery-solving."

"Which would be," Ed agreed, "the worst possible outcome."

"Wait a minute," Larkin said. "Are you making fun of me?"

"No," Ed said. "But you seemed a little down, so I figured I'd make some fun." He smiled at Larkin, his eyes crinkling. "Pun intended."

"I'm not down," Larkin said, which was only partially a lie. "I'm just thinking."

"About what?"

"About what I have to do to keep my job."

"You can't think like that," Ed said. "It keeps you from *doing* the job."

Larkin knew that Ed was right. He was an assistant professor of music at Howell College and had just begun the year-long process of securing tenure. By this time next year, Ed could be an associate professor at Howell, on his way to a full professorship—or he could be preparing to start over at another small liberal-arts college. He probably wouldn't end up being a barista, though. It probably wasn't even on his list of potential outcomes.

Not that Larkin had hated her job or anything, when she'd had it. The Coffee Shop was a good place to work, especially compared to some of the chain coffeehouses she'd slogged through in Los Angeles. But she'd earn less money, and she'd be less successful, and people wouldn't look at her the way Clarissa Bankshaw Morris had when she realized that Larkin was an Artistic Director.

"Hey," Ed said, nudging Larkin's shoulder. "We should get back."

"I should get back," Larkin said. "Pun intended."

"I don't get it," Ed said. "What's the pun?"

Larkin picked up her backpack. "Back to the person I was before I got distracted by all the things that could go wrong."

"Ah," Ed said. "Well, you know what you have to do."

That was true.

The trouble was that she didn't know how.

———

The afternoon did little to help Larkin come back from distraction. Isabella was sulking, and the only reason she wasn't telling everyone about how she had been unfairly dressed down was because she didn't want to admit she'd been caught with her clothes off. Everyone knew anyway —theater people always did, body language being their native tongue—and so Jiro was doing his best to pretend that it must all have been a terrible misunderstanding. Susan was taking Isabella's side, Stanley was standing by Jiro, and SuStan turned out to be completely useless as a pair of individuals. Not only did they spend the entire afternoon casting glances at each other, but the entire cast had to wait as Stanley went back to the mess hall for the measuring tape he had left behind.

"Sorry," he said, taking his place at the foot of the stage and the head of the Dress Parade. Each cast member would cross the stage in each of their successive costumes, allowing Stanley to both check and correct his work. It was the kind of activity that always took twice as long as anyone expected.

Swapping the sleeping potion yielded additional unexpected consequences. The larger bottle no longer fit into Juliet's girdle—and Larkin should have taken the time to measure the girdle before okaying the bottle, even though that was technically Isabella's job, or maybe Rebecca's job, but Rebecca didn't know and Isabella didn't care and Larkin was ultimately responsible for all of the technical aspects—and Susan and Stanley shouted back and forth about whether there would be time to make a larger girdle and whether it would be appropriate to the period.

"Could we give her a pocket?"

"Wrong century."

"We don't know that for sure. The word *pocket* first appeared in writing a hundred years before Shakespeare."

"But did any of those pockets appear *under women's dresses*?"

Velvet, sitting two seats away from Larkin and talking directly into the God Mic—a microphone that was connected to every speaker in the campground—stopped the argument. "Thank you, Susan, Stanley, let's move on.

The two of you can discuss your options and present a solution for Second Dress. For tonight, Farah can—"

As Stage Manager, Velvet had every right to make her own call; in fact, she should have. But Velvet, who had only ever worked in community theaters, looked to Larkin to learn what to do.

"She can carry the bottle in her hand," Larkin said, before remembering the blocking. "No, she can't. She can put the bottle in her girdle even though it's too big."

"No, she can't," Stanley said. "It'll tear the fabric."

"We can use the old bottle."

"I already put it away," Rebecca said.

"You can get it out again," Larkin said. "You can do that right now."

"No, she can't," Velvet said. "Rebecca can't walk to the prop shed alone."

Velvet had meant to whisper, but the God Mic picked it up anyway. The crackle of compressed air filled the amphitheater as Rebecca shifted miserably in her creaky plastic seat. Larkin sat silently, hoping somebody else would speak; she had made too many wrong guesses in succession, and didn't trust herself to contribute a solution.

"I'll walk with her."

It was, of course, Manny Morris. He'd been in the back row, watching the Dress Parade, for who knows how long. Nobody had bothered to tell Larkin.

"No, I'll walk with her."

That was Clarissa Bankshaw Morris. She was on the opposite side of the amphitheater, and Larkin watched Beatrix turn in surprise and then take out her phone. Manny must have announced his arrival in advance. Clarissa must not have—and Beatrix must have thought that it was important enough to text Sahil about, immediately, without even pretending to hide her secret internet access. The phone was just bright enough for Larkin to make out the message: *CBM is here too.*

Larkin turned to Velvet. "Camryn can walk with Rebecca. How long before our next break?"

Velvet, putting one hand over the God Mic just in case, turned towards her 18-year-old ASM.

"Twenty minutes," Camryn assisted.

"Take it now," Larkin directed.

————

After the break—a ten-minute interval in which Camryn and Rebecca went to retrieve the bottle, Susan and Stanley went to make separate conversations with Manny and Clarissa, Ed and Portia went to help Tyler work out some of his more complicated choreography in his Romeo costume, Beatrix went off to make a phone call, and Larkin remained exactly where she was—the Dress Parade continued. Supernumeraries, this time; sophomores and septuagenarians walking awkwardly in doublets and ruffs. Portia vaulted onto the stage, her hands propelling herself upwards like a gymnast, to instruct the cast in what she called an *Elizabethan promenade.*

"I know that's an anachronism," she called back, towards the newly bisected SuStan.

"I'll allow it," Susan replied.

This was where Stanley should have said *but I won't*— but he didn't, so Portia moved on. *Pun intended,* Larkin thought, and then wondered where Ed had gotten to. Where Beatrix had gotten to. Where Manny and Clarissa and Rebecca had gotten to. Where Isabella and Jiro had gotten to. Peg was up in the light booth—or at least Larkin assumed she was, since the lights kept changing. Velvet and Camryn were two seats away. Susan and Stanley were two rows apart.

"Every step is actually two separate movements," Portia said. "The first to transfer the weight. The second to secure it."

The supernumeraries, tottering on their chopines—the Elizabethan version of the platform shoe—began subdividing.

"Count it like an iamb," Portia said. She began reciting, in rhythm: "Be wary, look about. Be wary, look about."

Larkin looked, warily.

Velvet, Camryn, Susan, Stanley, Portia, Peg, and the cast.

Everyone else had gone.

CHAPTER 4

"Remind me how this one ends," Claire said, the off-duty police officer pushing her fingers through her sweaty auburn bob. "Happily ever after, right?"

"Actually," Josephine said, taking a sip of water from a reusable aluminum bottle before passing it to her girlfriend, "there have been many versions of *Romeo and Juliet* that have changed Shakespeare's ending. The most famous one is Prokofiev's ballet, of course."

"Of course," Claire said, teasing the former academic dean. "Everyone knows that."

"And during the Restoration," Josephine continued, extending her lecture to include Anni, Elliott, and Larkin, "Many productions of *Romeo and Juliet* were reworked as comedies of manners."

She paused, as if anticipating a question.

"All right," Elliott said. "I'll take one for the team. What is a comedy of manners?"

As Josephine launched into a brief history of the Stuart monarchy and its effect on English culture, Larkin noted the changes that had taken place since the beginning of the summer. Her mother looked more relaxed than Larkin had ever seen her. It was clear that Josephine Day was happier teaching poetry at the local library than helping to run a struggling liberal arts school. Claire, on the other hand, seemed to have absorbed some of the stresses that Josephine had put down. Larkin didn't know how much of this was related to Pal, Claire's aging, ailing golden retriever—and how much was related to Josephine's unexpected early retirement. She wondered if Claire felt financially responsible for their three-person household, even though Larkin was finally earning enough money to contribute as a peer. She wondered if Claire and her mother were worried about Larkin's money disappearing, if she moved out—or moved in with Ed.

Not that Ed had asked. Not that Larkin had asked him. Not that they wanted to. Not that they could live together even if they wanted to, because he still had to wait for his tenure application to be approved before he could start thinking long-term. Until then, Ed could live in his one-bedroom apartment and Larkin could live in her mother's guest bedroom and they could live vicariously through Anni and Elliott.

Larkin had already heard all about Anni and Elliott's house-hunting process. She hadn't paid as much attention as she should have, because she had been watching the way Anni and Elliott interacted with each other. Physical language was always much more revealing than spoken language, and these two young lovers—"middle-aged lovers," Anni had said, "since I'm about to turn thirty-nine and Elliott is forty-five"—were not hiding anything from anybody. Tiny towheaded Anni, who used to avoid human contact, had begun embracing it. Literally. The first thing Anni had done, when she had seen Larkin, was let go of her boyfriend's hand and run to give her best friend an enormous hug.

"I forgot you'd be sticky," Anni had said, detaching her face from Larkin's armpit and pulling a wet wipe out of her ever-present canvas utility bag. "We drove up in the air conditioning." She carefully wiped herself off, digging out a second wipe to disinfect her round-framed glasses, and offered the box to Larkin. "They're biodegradable, don't worry. Also they have sunscreen."

This was the Anni that Larkin remembered. Fastidious, unapologetic, always prepared. The Anni that Larkin did not yet know—"I don't know her either," Anni had said, "since I'm still becoming her"—was slowly rendering itself into recognition. This Anni appeared to be growing out her hair, and had fashioned a series of tiny barrettes to keep it out of her eyes. The barrettes had tiny skulls on them. "I know that's *Hamlet*," Anni had said, "but we don't have a good iconography for *Romeo and Juliet*. Should I have gone with stars? Hearts? Knives?"

Elliott still looked like Elliott, thank goodness. Still rangy, still ginger, still wearing a worn-out T-shirt that had some kind of nerd joke on it. He had driven everybody up in his bumper-sticker-covered car, and appeared to be chaperoning the evening.

"Where's Ed?" he asked, after Josephine finally got them from the Stuarts to the Hanovers.

"I don't know," Larkin said. She seemed to have lost track of what was important—she knew, for example, that she should be talking to Portia about helping Tyler with a bit of blocking that had become encumbered by his Romeo costume, or talking to Susan and Stanley about what they needed to do with Juliet's potion bottle, or talking to Beatrix about talking to Isabella about professional responsibilities, but then she'd have to tell Beatrix to have a similar conversation with Jiro, and she couldn't imagine that conversation ever taking place, and she wondered if the reason Jiro had become who he was had to do with years and years of *nobody ever having that conversation with him*—and then Ed said "Hello, Elliott," as if he had been there all along.

"How's the musical directing?" Elliott asked.

"Measure for measure," Ed said. "Pun intended." He put his arm around Larkin, but it was the wrong play; she could tell, by the way he squeezed her sweaty shoulder against his well-built chest, that Ed was also distracted. She didn't know what had gotten into his head, but it was coming out in his hands. His fingers, brushing against Larkin's forearm, felt *guilty*.

But that could just be Larkin's insecurity, transferring from her body to Ed's and back again. Her Best Self would put a stop to this speculation. "Shall we go inside?" she said, to the assembled group. She directed their attention towards the amphitheater with a gesture that was just a little too dramatic. "I mean, it's not really inside. It's an outdoor theater!" She laughed, a little too loudly. "It's like I haven't been working here all summer!"

That's exactly what it's like, Larkin thought. Like she'd gone back, somehow, to a second-best-self—and so, as they walked together into the wooden O, she held back to talk to Anni.

"How am I doing?" she whispered.

"How is the performance doing?" Anni whispered back.

"We'll find out," Larkin said, "two hours from now."

————

It ended up taking four hours, give or take, to get from *Romeo and Juliet's* famous prologue to its infamous ending. While Larkin had originally shared Shakespeare's optimism that the entire play could be completed in two hours' traffic, Sahil had encouraged her to stretch it to three. "Our audiences expect an event," he explained, "and our vendors expect two intermissions." This meant hiring people like Ed to rehearse a quartet of period-appropriate musicians, and hiring people like Portia to stage Morris dances and choreograph swordplay, and although Larkin wondered if they could have gotten the budget to balance a little better if they'd left out the viols and the gambols and the vendors altogether, she wasn't about to begrudge anyone their jobs. Nor was she going to begrudge The Coffee Shop its opportunity to sell people enough espresso to stay awake through Act V.

So it was a three-hour play, or it should have been. The extra hour came from the last-minute adjustments that always ended up stretching the first dress rehearsal to its seams—and snapping two stitches on Juliet's girdle, because Rebecca had neglected to remove the larger bottle from the props table and Farah had taken the wrong potion—but nothing had broken, not yet, and Juliet lay patiently in her tomb as Romeo sacked Paris.

The audience was equally patient, sitting quietly as Tyler executed his last bit of choreography. Larkin was in the center of the amphitheater, taking notes on her yellow legal pad. Velvet, as stage manager, had taken her place in the booth; Camryn, as assistant stage manager, had taken her place backstage. The remaining members of the production team were scattered throughout the auditorium. Ed and Portia near the front, to watch the fingering and the feet; Susan and Stanley in the back, with a few seats of disrespectful distance between them. Isabella and

Jiro were two rows ahead of Larkin; during the balcony scene, Isabella had allowed her head to rest against Jiro's shoulder and he had disallowed it with a single agitated twitch. Larkin didn't blame him; everyone else was watching Farah part the curtains of the balcony he had designed, and Isabella was making his moment about herself—although Larkin suspected that Isabella would have said that she was making it about the two of them.

But Larkin wasn't here to watch Isabella and Jiro. She was here to watch the production—and to pay careful attention to Anni, Elliott, her mother, and Claire. She had asked them all to sit directly in front of her, and had been tracking their responses since the play began. She was also watching the Malhotras, after quietly instructing Beatrix to seat them a few rows ahead of her family and friends. Sahil had seen the production before, in its various stages of progress. Sahil's wife, Dr. Rupa Malhotra, had not. Neither had their son, Jay, a surgical resident from Chicago who had driven home for a brief vacation. Larkin had not known that Sahil and Rupa had a son. She had assumed that they were one of those couples who produced instead of reproduced, and the existence of Jay—a winning combination of his mother's brains, his father's charm, and their shared enthusiasm for life—was prompting Larkin to rethink her entire life plan. *I could have something like that,* Larkin thought. *A family and a career. Something like Jay.*

She watched their son as he sat, his curly hair blowing slightly in the warm summer evening, and noted how carefully he was paying attention. She watched all of them: Jay and Rupa and Sahil and Beatrix, Claire and Josephine and Anni and Elliott. This was her first real test, as a director; to see if these people could suspend the belief that they'd seen this play before. That they knew how the story ended.

The truth was—as Larkin told herself, to tell Ed later—that none of them had seen this play before. Some of them had not yet seen this production, with Jiro's sets, Stanley's costumes, Portia's choreography, Peg's lighting, and Ed's music. Others had not yet seen how Larkin had integrated everything into a continuous series of rising and falling actions. But none of them—not a single person in the theater—had seen the action that was taking place in front of them, in the moment, regenerated from memory and reinvigorated with life. None of them knew how it would end. None of them knew, for sure, what would happen next.

That was why they kept watching.

Only Elliott, the former stage magician, suspected that Larkin was watching her audience along with her actors, to see where their interest rose and fell. "Are we giving you what you need?" he asked Larkin, at the first intermission.

"Yes," Larkin said, surprised that he would ask so openly—but that was Elliott, and that was why Anni loved him.

"Are you aware that the people in Row H want you to fail?"

"Yes," Larkin said again. Elliott was referring to Manny and Amelia, who had arrived together. He was also referring to Clarissa, who had enlisted Rebecca to sit with her—and then placed herself and her daughter next to her soon-to-be-ex-husband as if there were no other empty seats in the theater. Larkin had deliberately avoided looking over her left shoulder, even though she could feel three faces radiating hatred in her direction.

"The kid's different," Elliott continued. "She's on your side."

During the second intermission, Larkin asked Rebecca

to sit next to her. She also asked Peg, who had been walking up and down the aisles to view the lights from various angles, to join them—"just in case I need to get up for any reason," she explained. She didn't want anyone to accuse her of leaving Rebecca unsupervised, not when there were at least three people hoping she would make a fireable error.

"Sure," Peg said. "It'll give me a chance to say hi to Claire."

Larkin had forgotten that Peg and Claire had dated. She steeled herself for glares, but the three women—Peg, Claire, and Josephine—instantly behaved as old friends. By the time the actors were taking their places, Josephine had already invited Peg over for dinner.

"I'm sure you know how well Claire can cook," she said.

"I sure do," Peg agreed.

"I want to be like them when I grow up," Rebecca whispered to Larkin. She had tied a bandana around her thick, greasy hair; Larkin suspected that Peg had given it to her, and already knew that Rebecca's mother disapproved.

"You can be anything you want," Larkin said, because that was what you were supposed to say to seventeen-year-olds, even though they were old enough to know it wasn't true. That was the real difference between Rebecca and Juliet; Shakespeare's heroine, who had not yet seen the change of fourteen years, still believed that she could escape the panopticon that surrounded her.

And so Juliet, as played by the radiant Farah Emerson, awoke. Larkin had chosen to keep the brief interaction between Juliet and Friar Laurence—a moment that other directors cut, since it spoiled the intimacy of the two lovers in the tomb—and was rewarded by a surge of attention from her audience. *This isn't what I remember*, Larkin could see them thinking. *It wasn't in the movie. What's going on?*

Larkin knew exactly what was going to happen—the dismissal of the Friar, the admittance of the dagger—except this time Farah feinted the stabbing, driving the blade under her armpit instead of between her breasts. They heard fabric tear; they heard Stanley groan. Larkin thought about stopping the show to address whatever had gone wrong, but they were so close to the end—and so she let the Prince issue his final sentences, pardons and punishments, never a story of more woe, and so on.

She even let her audience applaud, even though her cast had not yet staged their bows. Curtain call was never blocked until right before the final dress, one of those traditions-cum-superstitions that held everyone together during these last hectic tech rehearsals. Velvet's call was next—"thank you cast, thank you crew, thank you production, thank you audience, let's take ten and meet on stage in costume for notes"—and as Larkin stood to hug Claire and twitch her nose at her mother and smile at Anni and nod at Elliott, she heard Farah call out from the stage.

"Someone fucked up the daggers," Farah said, her voice wild and wavering. She had maintained control until that very moment, and now she was losing it. "This was the real one. It had a blade. I could have stabbed myself."

"Thank you, Farah," Velvet said, the God Mic blanketing the amphitheater. "I'm sure it was an accident. We'll address it during notes."

"I could have died," Farah said, uncertain and agitated. She was Juliet, following the script, sitting in her own tomb and beginning to realize that something had gone terribly wrong. "Tyler could have died."

"Nobody died," Velvet corrected, calmly, "and Romeo never uses the dagger."

"Tyler," Farah said, balancing carefully on the edge of her slab and stretching her hand towards Romeo's body. "Sit up."

Larkin watched the moment.

They all did.

They all knew it was how the scene should have been staged.

They all wondered if there was time to restage it.

"What's in his hand?" Farah asked, looking out into the darkness. "Which bottle is this? What did he drink?"

And they all knew—Larkin watched them all realize it, together—that Tyler was dead.

CHAPTER 5

"Tell me again why you switched the bottles."

For the second time in her life, Larkin had been taken to the police station for questioning. This time, the officer facing her was not Claire Novak.

"I didn't switch the bottles." Larkin understood that her job was to provide information that could lead them to a suspect. She also understood that she could lose her job if she provided any information that led them to suspect *her*. "I requested that the bottles be swapped."

"Why?"

"Because the bottle we were using was too small to be seen from the back row."

"Then what happened?"

"My Props Master, Isabella Willis, found a larger bottle."

"Where did she find it?"

"I would assume she found it in the props shed, although I can't say for sure. I don't believe she went off camp to get it."

"Then what happened?"

"The bottle was too large to fit into Juliet's girdle." Larkin felt like she ought to offer a better explanation. "During Shakespeare's time, a girdle was a belt worn over the dress. Women tucked small objects inside their girdles for safekeeping."

"So you switched the bottles back."

"I requested that the bottles be swapped back," Larkin said, "and the task was assigned to Rebecca Bankshaw Morris, our Props Assistant." She tried to remember what, precisely, had happened. "And our Assistant Stage Manager, Camryn Kunkel."

"Did you confirm that the bottles had been swapped back?"

"No. Farah took the larger bottle onstage by mistake." If Larkin had been on her game, she would have looked at the props table before the first dress rehearsal. She would have asked Isabella to make an announcement to all of the actors, so that everybody knew which bottle was which. It could have empowered Isabella. It could have saved Tyler. Except—

"It wouldn't have mattered."

"What do you mean?" the investigator questioned.

"We're discussing the bottle Juliet carries with her in act 1. That's a completely separate bottle from the one Romeo carries in act 5." She wanted to explain that they were in completely different places on the Props Table, outlined in completely different pieces of electrical tape. The fact that Juliet's bottle had been swapped shouldn't have affected Romeo's bottle at all. Except—

"But you told the actors to expect different bottles."

"Not in those exact words." That was a lie. Larkin had passed that exact sentence, over and over in her mind, ever since Tyler had died. "Yes. I did create a situation in which my actors did not know what to expect on the Props Table."

"Did Tyler Mackintosh usually drink from the bottle he carried in act 5?"

"Yes."

"What was usually inside the bottle?"

"Traditionally, it's cold tea."

"What do you mean, traditionally?"

"I mean it's one of those things theater people do out of superstition. We could have put water inside the bottle, or apple juice, or literally anything, but a long time ago somebody started using cold tea, probably because it was the same color as whiskey or whatever it was substituting for, and now everybody does it." Larkin felt like she had to explain to the investigator how ridiculous this tradition was. "I don't mean iced tea. I mean hot tea, that the assistant props manager brews in advance and then lets cool. It's disgusting."

"Did you watch the assistant props manager brew the tea?"

"No," Larkin said. Somebody must have, since Rebecca was not allowed to do anything on her own, but she didn't feel like clarifying that point. "Nor did I watch anybody pour the tea into the bottles."

"Could anybody have accessed the teapot at any time?"

"Probably."

"Could anybody have accessed the Props Table at any time?"

"Probably."

"Could anybody have accessed the bottle Romeo uses in act 5 at any time?"

"Probably."

The investigator removed a glossy photograph from a

file folder and shoved it in Larkin's direction. *Just like the detectives on TV*, Larkin thought. "Prior to this evening," the investigator asked, "had you ever seen this bottle before?"

"Yes." It was a standard metal flask that had been wrapped in patterned leather to look Elizabethan. A leather strap allowed Romeo to wear the bottle when he wasn't drinking from it.

"Can you describe how this bottle is used in your production?"

"This is the bottle that Romeo carries onstage in act 5, scene 3. It is on his belt when he attacks and kills Paris." They had choreographed the scene to ensure the bottle remained on the downstage thigh, in full view of the audience.

"Are you certain that it is the same bottle?"

"Not absolutely certain," Larkin said, carefully, "but it would be very difficult to recreate this prop without significant effort. You could ask our costume designer, Stanley Levinstein, whether it was his leather work." Stanley had stitched together pieces of red and yellow leather, as a joke. Everything had been a joke to him.

"Was it the bottle that Tyler Mackintosh had been directed to drink from?"

"Yes." Other directors would have faked the drinking, asking their actors to guzzle air. Larkin had not, and Tyler had taken the bottle's contents in a single swallow. Even if he had realized something was wrong, it would have been too late.

"Do you know what was inside the bottle?"

"Only because Dr. Rupa Malhotra told me." The diagnosis had been as instant as the death, and as obvious. "Cold tea and cyanide."

———

"He didn't ask me why the daggers were swapped," Larkin said, after the interrogation had ended. Her mother had taken her home. Everyone had agreed that it was too late to drive back to the campsite. Larkin had showered, and put on a pair of pajamas she hadn't worn since May. "That's the most important question."

"Why is it the most important question?" Anni asked. The two of them were sitting in Larkin's bedroom. Elliott was with Josephine and Claire, keeping calm and company in the living room. Everybody was pretending that they were going to go to bed soon.

"Because it means someone wanted to murder both Romeo and Juliet."

Anni considered this. "They wanted Romeo to poison himself for real, and Juliet to stab herself for real."

"Yes," Larkin said. It was the only thing that made sense, except for the part where *it didn't make any sense.*

"What's the motive?"

"I don't know." Larkin sipped her coffee. It was after midnight when they all got home and the first thing her mother had done was start a pot of coffee. Anni was drinking chamomile tea. She'd brought the tea in her bag, just in case. She'd also brought a change of clothes, which meant she was sitting next to Larkin in a T-shirt that read *What does C# mean to you?* It looked like one of Elliott's, and Anni had already tucked both her knees and her feet inside.

"Do you think somebody was out to get the Shakespeare Festival?"

"Like, were they trying to shut us down?" Larkin shook her head. "No. Why would they do that? What would be the point?"

"Old white men glorifying cultures that aren't their own?"

"First of all," Larkin said, "Shakespeare was my age when he wrote *Romeo and Juliet*. Second of all, the star-crossed lovers story appears in multiple cultural narratives. It's part of the collective unconsciousness, like the quest story." She knew there had to be another example. "The story of the great flood."

"The story of how we got banished from paradise by taking what we hadn't earned," Anni said, "or by taking shortcuts instead of doing the work."

"Right." There was something more to that—there was always something more to everything Anni said—but Larkin couldn't think of what it was. She kept hearing Rebecca's three-syllable *ban-ish-ed*. She wondered what Ed was doing. He had stayed on camp, to prepare the cast for what would have to happen the next day. The police investigation; the second dress rehearsal.

"So we can check *upset that we're doing Shakespeare* off the list," Anni said. She opened her canvas bag and took out a notebook with a pink-and-purple cover. "We can also check off *upset that Shakespeare set a play in Italy even though he'd never been there.*"

"Yes," Larkin said. "Nobody is doing this to protest Shakespeare's lack of cultural sensitivity." Shakespeare was more sensitive to the human condition than most playwrights. That's why they were still doing his plays—that, and the fact that you didn't have to pay a licensing company to use them.

Anni wrote both items in her notebook and then crossed them both off. "What if it's the other way around? What if someone is upset that you cast a Middle Eastern Juliet?" Anni began writing, then stopped. "Is she Iranian?"

"Actually, yes," Larkin said. "Her mother's family got out before the revolution." Farah had told the story to everyone during their first cast-and-crew campfire. "Her father's white. An accountant, or something. They live in New York." Anni continued writing. "You don't think—"

"It's a possibility."

"That somebody is out to get Juliet because we cast a woman of Iranian descent?"

"Not necessarily," Anni said. "But I do think somebody is out to get Farah Emerson."

"Why?"

Anni showed Larkin her notebook. "The poison worked," she said, tapping the part of the page that read *POISON*, "but the dagger didn't." Anni circled the word *DAGGER* three times. "Juliet survived, even though she wasn't supposed to." She wrote one more sentence in her notebook and passed it to Larkin.

"The problem isn't that Tyler Mackintosh died," Larkin read aloud. "Wait, Anni—"

"I know," Anni said. "Tyler's death is a problem. But it's not the real problem."

"The problem is that Farah Emerson is still alive."

———

"I really don't see that being a problem," Sahil said, the next morning. They were in his office, in Cedar Rapids. Larkin was wearing yesterday's clothing; somebody—she suspected either Claire or Elliott—had washed and folded it while she slept. Jay Malhotra was sitting on the credenza, by the window, as if he had nothing better to do than watch his father determine the fate of the Festival.

"I've already arranged everything with Beatrix," Sahil explained. "She and Camryn and Rebecca will conduct a props audit before every performance, and will re-audit the props table after each intermission. We are no longer using any consumable liquids in any of the bottles. All of the drinking and swallowing will be pantomimed, and all of the bottles will be made of clear plastic." He cleared his throat. "Beatrix also purchased two matching prop daggers with retractable plastic blades."

"SuStan will hate that," Larkin said. "The daggers won't look period." She wondered if getting them to agree on something would solve their relationship issues. Then she tried to think of a better solution. "You could ask the community theater if they could lend us anything."

"We will not be getting any of the community theaters involved," Sahil said. He glanced, a little guiltily, at his son. "Larkin, you understand that we have a unique opportunity here."

That kind of sentence never presaged good news. Sahil raked his hand through his thinning hair—Larkin immediately understood where Jay had picked up the gesture— and continued. "We're bringing Summer Shakespeare back from hiatus. We had to cancel it, the entire thing, for three years running. We will not be canceling it now."

This sounded like the kind of statement that should have been issued with a little more optimism. Instead, Sahil looked shamefully at the corner of his antique rug, his foot twitching a bit of fringe into submission. "We have a unique opportunity," he said again.

"What my father is trying to say," Jay said, leaving his perch and taking his place in the center of the room, "is that nobody has to know what happened last night."

"How are you going to keep people from finding out?" Larkin asked. She had been surprised, when Elliott drove her to Sahil's office, that the receptionist hadn't mentioned it. That people hadn't been whispering about it in the elevator. That she had made it all the way to the fourteenth floor without hearing a word about Tyler Mackintosh's death.

"We aren't going to keep anybody from doing anything," Jay said. "It's going to happen naturally."

Then Larkin understood. "Nobody on camp has access to the internet."

"Which means no social media posts," Jay said.

"The cabins don't even have electricity," Larkin said. "Nobody's been charging their phones." A few people had tried, the first few days, carrying their phones into the mess hall to look for available outlets—but the coffee machine and the toaster took precedence, and by the end of the first week all of the inessential electronic devices had been shoved into the recesses of backpacks or the creases of duffel bags.

"Which means no recordings," Jay said. "No photographs. No opportunity to share what happened."

"Handwritten letters," Larkin said.

"I've asked Beatrix to hold the mail," Sahil said.

"Landline phone calls," Larkin said.

"I've asked Beatrix to disable the mess hall phone."

"The police report in the newspaper." Larkin was thinking, carefully, of everything that happened after a death. "The obituary."

"They won't run right away," Sahil said, "and even if they did, nobody reads the newspaper anymore."

"People will find out," Larkin said. "It will be impossible to keep Tyler Mackintosh's death a secret."

"I know," Sahil said. "But we have the opportunity to control the narrative." He shifted himself into the kind of stance that would have looked authoritative if his left foot wasn't still twitching the rug. "We will complete our two remaining dress rehearsals. We will hold our preview performance. By then the news will have reached—"

"The mainland?" Larkin filled in. Jay, who had stepped aside when his father began his speech, smiled at her. He might even have winked. Then he used his right heel to nudge a bit of antique rug fringe out of place.

"Yes," Sahil said, stepping to the spot his son had deliberately disarrayed. He bent over, this time, pulling each strand straight. "You understand that Preview Night is the most essential part of our mission."

"I thought our mission was to provide the kind of artistic experience that would anchor the Creative Corridor, give our community an affordable way to gather with friends and family, and allow our talented young people to build their skills by working alongside professionals."

"Yes," Sahil said again. "But that's only part of it. The preview, you must understand—"

He turned to look at Larkin, his left hand planting itself on the floor as counterbalance. "Larkin, our preview performance is the most essential financial part of the mission."

Once again, Larkin immediately understood. Preview Night was invitation-only. It was catered, with white jackets and silver trays. Larkin had already purchased the dress she would need to wear, to give the speech she would need to give before the show. She'd be standing in front of business owners, retired lawyers, startup founders. Strategic planners. Wealth managers. Impeccably dressed first wives; inappropriately dressed second ones. Eligible sons and daughters, matches made by candlelight. They were ostensibly there for the Shakespeare. They were really there to connect with each other, and to thank the Festival for helping them make those connections by making a donation or becoming a sponsor.

"Preview Night is when we begin to control the narrative," Larkin said. This time Jay's smile suggested that he had underestimated her. "You may have heard," she continued, as if she were already standing in front of her well-heeled crowd, "that the Summer Shakespeare Festival experienced a tragic death two days ago."

"Three," Jay said. "It'll be three."

"You may also have heard the phrase *the show must go on*."

"Yes," Sahil said. "Make sure you use those words."

"We understand the importance of bringing Shakespeare to our audiences, many of whom will be unaware of this unexpected and unprecedented event."

"Unprecedented," Jay said. "Good choice."

"We'd like to thank Caleb Alderton, our understudy, for stepping into the role of Romeo," Larkin said, "and assure you that we are working with local law enforcement to thoroughly investigate the circumstances—"

"No," Sahil said. "No mention of law enforcement."

"But Tyler was poisoned," Larkin said. "Your wife confirmed it."

"Rupa offered her medical opinion," Sahil corrected. "It is not yet fact."

"Well, let's say that she turns out to be right," Larkin said—and she watched Jay glance at her a third time. He was not used to seeing people stand up to his father. "Let's say somebody put cyanide in Romeo's poison bottle. Let's say that same person swapped Juliet's dagger. That person is very likely someone in the cast, or in the crew, or on the production team."

She stared down Sahil. "I have a murderer in my company, and I'm still allowing the show to go on?" Jay shook his head, slightly. Larkin asked herself *what Sahil wanted*—and then she asked herself *what Sahil feared*. "How long do you think it'll take the brightest business minds in the Creative Corridor to figure that one out?"

Sahil's face blanched—but he didn't flinch.

"Not if you figure it out first," he whispered. "By Preview Night."

"You want me to solve Tyler Mackintosh's murder," Larkin said.

"To save the Festival," Sahil said.

"No," Larkin said. She was uninterested in Sahil Malhotra's business interests, and she needed him to know that. "But I'll do it to save Farah."

———

Larkin's car was still on camp, so Jay offered to drive her back. His father had argued that Beatrix could be fetched, but Jay had said something about Beatrix needing to remain at the Festival to ensure nobody misplaced anybody else's props, and then he was escorting Larkin into a parking garage and opening the passenger side door for her. Moving the seat back without her having to ask.

Which meant that Larkin had to ask something else.

"Okay," she said, as soon as the doors were closed and the belts were buckled and the car was circling the parking garage helix towards its exit. "What's your deal?"

"She has a death to cover up and a killer to uncover," Jay mused—Larkin swore he winked at her again—"and she asks me what my deal is."

"No, seriously," Larkin said. She hadn't slept well. Her skin was prickly. The tightness around her face should have made her tired, but she felt alert. Alive. "You're kind of a jackass. Sorry."

"I don't believe white women are allowed to call brown men jackasses," Jay said.

"I said sorry," Larkin said.

"White women are always allowed to be sorry for things," Jay said, "so I will accept your apology."

He paused at a stoplight; turned right towards the highway.

"But—if you don't mind, it's a twenty-minute drive, we'll have to talk about something—were you apologizing because you don't really believe I'm a jackass? Or because you do?" Jay smiled, with intent, and shifted his car into a higher gear. "Because I kind of am." The sudden acceleration pushed Larkin backward. Her seat belt tightened. They passed the speed limit sign. "Although you should know that I've spent much of my adult life trying not to be."

"That's why you went into medicine, like your mother," Larkin said, "instead of business, like your father."

"My mother said I would like you," Jay said. "She said you were very smart, and very good with people." He shifted the car into the left lane. "She also said you would not like me."

"Because you're good with people the way your father is," Larkin said. "The business way."

"It has nothing to do with business," Jay said. "Just like yours has nothing to do with theater. You and I both know how to get other people to do what we want." He shifted back to the right, the cars behind them receding into the background. "But when you do it, nobody calls you a jackass afterwards."

"I told you I was sorry!" Larkin said. She wondered if Jay was trying to get her to do something. Feel badly, probably, for assessing him so correctly. "And I like your dad. I don't know why you manipulated him, in his office."

"Who says I was manipulating him?" Jay asked.

"You were messing with his rug!" Larkin said. "You were deliberately putting him in a humiliating position! He was bent over, on the floor—"

Then she figured it out.

"You were manipulating me. You wanted me to feel sorry for him. It didn't work." That wasn't quite true. "I mean, it did, but I really felt angry."

"White women love feeling sorry when they really feel angry," Jay said again. "And now you're going to solve the murder and save the Festival."

"I'm going to save Farah," Larkin said again.

"And your job."

Jay turned off the highway and towards the campsite. White lines became yellow; blacktop became gravel.

"You didn't become a doctor because you wanted to be like your mother," Larkin said. She was on her game again, and two could play. "Rupa's a pediatrician. You're a surgeon."

"Lead surgical resident," Jay said, "and you have to understand that there are only three career paths for a second-generation Indian boy with extremely wealthy parents. Doctor-lawyer-business, right?" He shook his head, rapid and relaxed, from side to side. "I picked doctor. Extremely wealthy doctor."

"Yes," Larkin said, "and you never told anybody why. You told your mother you were doing it to help people. You told your father you were doing it to make money. You're really doing it because you wanted something you could manipulate without hurting people. Life itself, not products or computers or the legal system. That's why you didn't go into law or business, even though you would have been very good at both. You're afraid of who you could be, if you didn't try to be God. You wouldn't be a jackass. You'd be the Devil."

The car paused, then stopped, in the parking lot.

"Well done," Jay said. "They told me you were a detective."

"What else did they tell you?" Larkin asked.

"Jaipal Malhotra," Jay said, in his mother's voice, "you cannot fall in love with this girl."

CHAPTER 6

"How does someone become a murderer?"

Larkin and Ed glanced at each other. They had gone the entire day—the entire second dress rehearsal—without anyone saying that word aloud.

"I don't know, Rebecca," Ed said. He took a squat next to Rebecca's bunk, eyes level with hers, just close enough to be avuncular. "Sometimes people do things without thinking carefully."

"Murderers think very carefully," Rebecca said. "Everyone knows that." She looked as if she wanted to cry. Ed looked as if he wanted to squeeze her shoulder. Neither of them moved.

"Well," Ed said, "sometimes people think they're thinking carefully, but they're actually thinking selfishly. They want something, and they're willing to hurt someone to get it."

"Murderers are willing to kill someone," Rebecca said. "Everyone knows that." She looked at Larkin, seeking answers instead of uncles. "You know why people murder people. How do they decide to do it?"

Larkin thought, carefully.

"This is why we do theater," she finally said. "To understand how a person becomes who they become. Why they make the decisions they make. How the people around them affect their choices."

She sat on Rebecca's bunk. It smelled like the end of the day, armpits and feet and flatulence, the body releasing its burdens before sleep. Larkin had written a paper in college —citing zero sources, claiming original research—about how you could tell a person's mental state from the odor of their bedding. Rebecca's had gotten stronger, since Larkin had last been in the cabin. She had been the only company member brave enough to call Tyler's death by its real name.

"We still don't even know what happened to our Romeo," Ed said. That was cowardly—*cow-ar-ed-ly*, Larkin thought, without thinking—but fair. She had told Ed what Rupa had told her after Tyler's death. She had told Ed what Sahil had told her that morning. She had asked Ed not to mention cyanide to anyone, and he hadn't. But he hadn't called Tyler by his name, either. It was *un-ex-pect-ed*.

"Are you going to solve the murder?" Rebecca asked.

Larkin couldn't say yes, not directly—so she turned the conversation in a different direction. "There are three questions you need to ask, if you want to understand how somebody becomes a murderer. Who did it, how they did it, and why they did it."

She picked up Rebecca's copy of *Romeo and Juliet* and handed it over. "Who killed Tybalt? I mean, in the play."

"Romeo."

"How did Romeo kill Tybalt?"

"With a sword."

"Is that in the text?" It was the kind of question she

used to ask, when she was a grad student teaching Theater 101.

She watched Rebecca open—and follow—her script. "No."

"How did Romeo kill Tybalt?" Larkin asked again.

"It doesn't say."

"What does it say?"

"They fight," Rebecca read aloud. "Tybalt falls."

"So we don't know for sure how it was done," Larkin said. "The director could make a choice, for example, to have Romeo and Tybalt use guns." She wondered if Rebecca were old enough to have seen the Baz Luhrmann movie. Maybe high schools didn't show it, anymore. They'd stopped showing the Franco Zeffirelli film as soon as they'd had an option that didn't include full frontal nudity. "Or Romeo and Tybalt could get into a physical fight."

"Okay," Rebecca said. She looked a little embarrassed, to be caught out at misunderstanding Shakespeare—so Larkin gave her a chance to redeem herself.

"Did Romeo kill Tybalt on purpose?"

Rebecca consulted her copy, reading aloud:

"Now, Tybalt, take the villain back again,

That late thou gavest me; for Mercutio's soul

Is but a little way above our heads,

Staying for thine to keep him company:

Either thou, or I, or both, must go with him."

She put her finger in the page and looked at Larkin. "Yes," she said. "Romeo tells Tybalt they're going to fight until one or both of them are dead."

"Why does Romeo decide to do this?" Larkin asked. This was, perhaps, the most important question in the entire play. It was also the most important question in their current production. *Why had one of them become a murderer? What had prompted that decision?*

Rebecca took her finger out of her Shakespeare and turned a few pages back. "Because Tybalt killed Mercutio," she said, giving the right answer while looking for a better one. "But Tybalt isn't a murderer. It's kind of like this terrible mistake."

"Tybalt challenges Romeo to a duel," Larkin says, "because Romeo has insulted the Capulet family honor by crashing their party."

"Even though Lord Capulet tells him not to do it," Ed adds. "He likes Romeo and is ready to make amends with the Montagues." This was another aspect of the play that many directors overlooked; another moment that Larkin had insisted her audience pay attention to.

"And Romeo says he won't fight Tybalt," Rebecca continues, "and he's about to tell Tybalt that he and Juliet got secret-married, and then Mercutio interrupts them."

"And Mercutio says he's going to fight Tybalt instead," Larkin says, "and then he dies."

Rebecca read her page very carefully. "They fight with swords," she finally said. "That's in the text."

"Right," Larkin said.

"But it doesn't say how Mercutio dies. It doesn't even say Tybalt stabbed him."

"Do you stab, with swords?" Ed asked, making a joke out of Rebecca's discovery. Larkin *ig-nor-ed* him.

"This is essential to understanding Shakespeare," Larkin said, keeping her focus on Rebecca so Rebecca could stay focused. "Mercutio's death could be viewed as accidental, depending on your reading of the scene. If you go back to the First Folio, it's deliberately unclear whether Tybalt meant for Mercutio to die. Subsequent printings include editorial stage directions that turn Tybalt into a murderer, but Shakespeare's original text leaves it ambiguous."

Larkin had also left it ambiguous. She knew, of course, what Tybalt had meant to do. So did the actor playing Tybalt. Her audience, she hoped, would enjoy discussing the possibilities—unless they spent both intermissions asking each other about the actor who should have been playing Romeo.

"Was Romeo supposed to die, in the duel?" Rebecca asked. "Or was he just supposed to lose the fight and go away?"

Now Larkin was embarrassed. "I don't know," she said. Everything she knew about the rules of dueling came from *Hamilton*. It might have been different, in Shakespeare's day.

"If Tybalt meant to kill Romeo," Rebecca said, "it makes Romeo a different kind of murderer."

"Why?"

"Because his decision to kill Tybalt is based on different reasons," Rebecca said. "It's about protecting his family, not avenging his friend."

"Maybe we should ask Susan," Larkin said, "tomorrow." She began an overdramatic yawn, but the joke became all too real as soon as she opened her mouth. She was more tired than she realized. "Tonight, we sleep."

"Perchance to dream," Ed said.

"Wrong play," Larkin and Rebecca said simultaneously.

After that, they turned out the lights, wishing each other goodnight in various appropriate ways; after that, Larkin pulled her sleeping bag over her head and turned her flashlight on.

Dear Anni,

You won't get this until after the previews, but I'm writing it anyway.

I'm no closer to figuring out whodunit than I was last night, even though I spent the entire day asking people how they were doing. "Were you okay giving your statement to the police?" "Are you ready for tonight's dress rehearsal?" "Do you want to talk about what happened?" Everyone was doing fine. Everyone was ready. Everyone wanted the show to go on.

Nobody wanted to talk about what had happened.

Instead, they want to say things like "it was a terrible accident" and "he must have been allergic to something, was it bees???" and "maybe he had a heart condition." Somebody suggested heatstroke. I know that Rupa didn't, like, bellow "IT WAS POISON" from the stage, she told me in private, but the fact that nobody is saying the word POISON—

And nobody is saying the word MURDER—

And I get it, if they were seriously worried for their own safety they wouldn't be here right now. I think. I don't know why they're here. I don't know why I'm here, since I'm one of the few people who knows that somebody on camp has access to cyanide. I can't even look up "how do you get cyanide" because I don't have access to the internet. I can't even send this to you because Beatrix is holding the mail until after the murder is solved.

The cast doesn't know this, of course. Nor do they know why we're no longer using consumable liquids onstage. An enormous Hy-Vee truck arrived this afternoon full of individually packaged water bottles, coffee bottles, iced tea bottles, sandwiches, chips, carrot sticks—you get the idea. Beatrix told everyone it was a gift, from Sahil, so they could focus on the dress rehearsals instead of preparing meals and cleaning the kitchen. Everyone is so thrilled to be off KP that nobody is asking why they're only allowed to drink from factory sealed containers.

Or maybe they're all asking, but nobody wants to talk about it with me. I'm the boss, and they all want to keep their jobs.

The one person who hates his job right now is Caleb Alderton. Romeo's understudy. You can lecture me about project management contingencies later, but we were supposed to have a few more understudy rehearsals than we actually did, and now Caleb is underprepared and overwhelmed.

Farah is also nervous as hell, and I don't blame her. She knows the swapped dagger was meant for her. The fact that she isn't going around saying this to everybody is either a sign of her professionality or, like, maybe she's worried that if she lets people know that SHE KNOWS SHE WAS SUPPOSED TO DIE—

But nobody's talking about the dagger. Not even Rebecca, who just asked me a bunch of questions about what makes someone decide to murder someone else. She knows that somebody killed Tyler, and I think she's also trying to figure out who it is.

Of course there is an obvious suspect, but it's never the obvious suspect. Amelia Jorgensen had enough momentum to throw herself at our former director without understanding it would take them both down. She could have had enough ambition to kill—but it only explains the swapped dagger. It doesn't explain why she poisoned Tyler, and Amelia should be smart enough to understand that I would never recast her in the role of Juliet if Farah Emerson were dead.

Kiss your boy and buy your house. I'll solve this. I have to.

Larkin

She pulled her head out of her sleeping bag—and saw Beatrix, on the opposite bunk, her face illuminated by her phone. Her dark hair did not cover her eyes; her glasses reflected a series of texts, gray and blue blocks replacing each other as she tapped her screen.

"Tell Sahil I want the internet," Larkin whispered.

She watched Beatrix send the message. She watched the reversed response 'slide up Beatrix's lenses. She watched Beatrix shake her head.

"He says it'll be a distraction."

"Then ask him to ask Rupa how someone could have brought cyanide to camp."

Beatrix jerked her eyes towards Larkin, fear glinting above her glasses frames. She hadn't known that was how Tyler died. Even if she'd suspected he'd been poisoned, which she must have done at least once while buying all of the single-use supplies, she hadn't asked herself which one —and Sahil, in his effort to control the narrative, hadn't told her.

As Beatrix texted the request, Larkin added a P.S. to her letter, scrawling it on what she hoped was the bottom of the page, not wanting to turn her flashlight on.

I figured it out

Not who did it

But maybe how to get them to reveal themselves

Tonight, she'd sleep—for the first time in two days. Tomorrow, she'd spend the last hours before the final dress rehearsal playing Hamlet. Putting a three-syllable poison into people's ears—*cy-an-ide*—and catching their consciences, one by one.

CHAPTER 7

"So here's something I've been wondering," Larkin said, popping the tab off her second can of coffee, "ever since I first read this play."

It was the morning of the final dress rehearsal. The mess hall, littered with the detritus of tamper-proof packaging. The production team, seated around their usual table. A lie, told to discover who knew the truth.

"Was there actually a sleeping potion that could have simulated death?" Larkin asked. "Or did Shakespeare make it all up?"

She knew the answer, of course—but she let someone else provide it.

"Belladonna," said Isabella. Of course the graduate student would be fastest with the answer—especially since it gave her the chance to prove that she was smarter than her director.

"Actually, any of the deadly nightshades could have worked," Susan said.

"The potato?" Stanley asked, dogging her. "The tomato?"

"Yes," Susan said, unwilling to pony up. "If enough atropine were extracted."

"What about the poison?" Larkin asked. "The one Romeo buys from the apothecary. It's a powder, right? The apothecary tells him to mix it with water."

"He says 'Put this in any liquid thing you will,'" Susan corrected. "There was a general lack of clean drinking water in the Elizabethan era. People drank wine and beer."

"What about tea?" Portia asked.

"An excellent method of killing the parasites in your local water supply," Susan said, "but it will be another fifty years before tea arrives in England."

"Wow," Isabella said. "And tea is, like, such a British thing."

"Yes," Susan said. "That's why the expression is *all the tea in Britain.*"

Jiro, who was Japanese, looked at Isabella with disgust. Beatrix, whose grandparents had emigrated from Shanghai to Chicago, was too distracted to care. She knew where Larkin was trying to take the conversation. She knew which neurotoxin Larkin was attempting to release.

"My mother used to say *all the café in New Orleans,*" Portia said, compressing the name of the city into two elegant syllables. "But coffee came after tea, if I recall?"

"It'll be a hundred years before we get to coffee," Susan said. "The dawn of the Enlightenment."

"*Coffee, coffee muss ich haben,*" Ed sang. "Bach, in 1735. He did an entire cantata on the problems coffee was causing in families. All the young people wanted to go off to the coffeehouses and talk, and drink, and think—you know there's this argument that we didn't really start thinking rationally until we started drinking coffee—and all of their parents wanted them to stay at home."

"Just like now," Rebecca whispered to Larkin.

"Just like Shakespeare," Larkin whispered back.

"You can't seriously argue that we didn't start thinking rationally until we started consuming brain-altering levels of caffeine," Portia said. "Was Aristotle irrational? Was Confucius? Was Saint Paul?"

"Saul was a kid from Tarsus who got caught up in the wrong crowd," Stanley said. "Sold out his people to escape, what? A little death?"

"Many would argue that Saul, or Paul, or Saint Paul, made an absolutely rational decision," Susan said, her liquid *u* dripping with venom. "Not only did he remain alive, but he was also able to contribute a body of documents that provided an essential foundation for both Christian faith and Western philosophy."

"And did he think, even once, about how that would play out for the Jews?" Stanley was getting heated. "Little Saulie wrote us off and you know it."

"Is it rational to preserve one's heritage?" Jiro asked. "To maintain familial bonds at the expense of a greater contribution?"

"Greater for you, or greater for the greater good?" Stanley retorted, dripping with sweat and condescension. "If Saul of Tarsus had been a utilitarian, he would have refused the call to become Saint Paul and saved us a couple of genocides."

"Someone else would have taken his place," Susan said, quietly. "The ideas were not his own, after all."

"You know," Peg said, "my uncle was a utilitarian minister." She stood up, carefully folding the plastic that had wrapped her apple. "All of his services ended with cookies, pie, doughnuts—you know, the greatest baked goods." Her joke fell flat, but it broke the tension. "Becks," she said, "want to come help me pack up some gels?"

Rebecca nodded, eagerly. "Yep," she said, sounding

like the kid she still was; the seventeen-year-old aching for something real to do and someone real to notice.

"I thought it was Unitarian," Isabella said. Susan stared. Jiro glared. Rebecca waved goodbye, and as Larkin watched her assistant prop master walk away with her lighting designer, she wished she'd had the forethought to match them up beforehand. Rebecca could have had a very different summer.

Beatrix, meanwhile, was still waiting for the remainder of the production team to have a different conversation. "You were going to say what powder it was," she said, turning to Larkin. "That the apothecary gave Romeo."

Larkin had been going to ask what powder it was, so that she could observe everybody's reactions when she revealed that it might have been cyanide, but Beatrix was too agitated to register the difference. "I looked it up," she said, forgetting that people weren't supposed to know she had internet. "Shakespeare knew. Everyone knew. There was only one thing that could kill Romeo that quickly—"

"Bea, love," a newly familiar voice called out. "Don't spoil the ending."

It was Jay, standing by the messy production table as if he had always been there. Larkin looked first to Jay, then to her team. Susan and Stanley knew him; they'd probably watched Jay grow up. It was hard to tell whether Stanley didn't like him or whether Stanley just didn't like anything at the moment; Susan found him intriguing. So did Isabella, who was staring at Jay like she'd never seen a grown man before. Jiro considered taking this personally —Larkin watched him consider it—and then decided to give her up.

"Jaipal Malhotra," Jay said, offering his hand to Isabella to get her to close her mouth. Larkin watched Isabella sparkle under Jay's gaze, and wondered once again *what his deal was*. It wasn't like Jay was particularly attractive or anything. He was the kind of man Larkin used to see every day when she went into the Summer Shakespeare offices in Cedar Rapids. A forehead that bore the weight of too many expensive decisions; a figure that bore the weight of too many expensive dinners. Good hair. Great clothes. A compelling smile. Jiro was better-looking, overall. Ed was *way* better looking—but Ed was the only member of the production team who hadn't turned towards Jay when he arrived. Instead, he'd turned towards Portia. The two of them were talking, on their own, having an entire conversation that didn't involve anyone else. They were getting up, wadding up compostable oatmeal packets and stuffing plastic wrap into empty water bottles.

"We're going to do some movement work with Farah and Caleb," Portia said. Larkin hadn't realized, at the beginning of the summer, how Ed would become part of Portia's process. He hadn't had enough to do, as musical director, so he'd begun helping Portia teach people how to count. Clapping out rhythms, or playing them at the piano. Larkin had seen it happen. She'd loved it, at the time—because she'd loved *him*. Ed had been his best self. They had been their best selves, together; Ed-and-Larkin, and Ed-and-Portia.

Now Ed was something else. More importantly, Ed-and-Portia were something else. Not collaborators, but conspirators. They were hiding something from Larkin, and they were gone before she had time to ask.

"Shall we follow them?" Jay said, his voice a breath ahead of Larkin's thoughts. "I know you want to."

"No," Larkin said. "If there's anything for Ed to tell me, he'll say it at lunch." She faced Jay, who was exactly her height—which was unusual, nobody was ever exactly her height, she wondered if Jay was wearing lifts in his boat shoes—and staked her claim. "On our date."

"All right," Jay said, smiling. Sweeping his hand through his hair. "I wasn't really feeling like playing spies. Too hot. Why did anyone think that staging a three-hour play outdoors in July was a good idea?"

"You know why," Larkin said. "Or you're smart enough to figure it out. Joseph Papp, in New York, in 1954."

"Ah, yes," Jay said. "The man who gave us Shakespeare in the Park."

"And then we all took it," Larkin said, "because parks are inexpensive and Shakespeare is free, even though the weather in New York, in the summer, in the 1950s, was way different than the weather in Eastern Iowa right now."

"And we built million-dollar amphitheaters," Jay said, "so we aren't even saving any money." He smiled again. "But you and I, Larkin—we're saving lives."

"So you also believe the murderer is going to strike again," Larkin said. With Jay, it seemed best to get to the point as quickly as possible. "Because they didn't hit their target the first time."

"Poor little Tyler Mackintosh," Jay said. "Just about to turn Equity, too."

Larkin didn't feel bad that Jay didn't feel bad for Tyler. She felt bad because he knew she didn't. She hadn't had time; she'd been lost in thoughts of saving Farah. Solving the mystery. Training an understudy. Directing a play. Tyler had been collateral damage, in both the literal and the figurative sense. She'd arrange a ceremony for him later, so everyone would have the chance to feel everything that they were putting off in order to put on a show. Ask Beatrix to arrange it, maybe.

Ask—"Why did you stop Beatrix from talking about cyanide?"

"Why did you want her to bring it up?"

"Because then I could watch everybody's reactions," Larkin said. "Like, when I mentioned cyanide to Beatrix last night it was obvious that she had no idea that was how Tyler had been killed. So I figured that if I mentioned it to everybody, you know—"

"Somebody would turn white?" Jay asked. "Reveal their guilt? Run screaming from the scene, like Hamlet's evil uncle Claudius?"

"It would have worked," Larkin said. "Somebody would have given something away."

"Perhaps," Jay said. "But did things go better or worse for Hamlet after he asked everyone in Denmark to consider that his father might have been poisoned?"

Larkin knew the answer. She should have known it before. "Worse."

"Yes," Jay said. "Hamlet reveals his knowledge too early. He wins information but loses the advantage." He spoke, carefully and quietly, into Larkin's ear. "It's the wrong move."

"What's the right one?" Larkin asked, just as carefully. She wasn't sure whether she could trust Jay. She was pretty sure Jay didn't trust her. The air had changed, since he arrived. Less humid. A cool, insistent wind that swept up the stray bits of leftover breakfast packaging. There would be *weather*, as they said in Iowa, *soon*.

"You wanted to know how somebody could have gotten their hands on potassium cyanide," Jay said. "I got the message, and am here to deliver it."

"You drove all the way out here?" Larkin asked. "Just for that?"

"You thought my father would allow the answer to be

sent via email?" Jay laughed. "When he got Beatrix's text, the one where you told her to *ask him to ask my mother*—well, my father considered destroying his phone."

Sahil would have had to delete his entire online presence, as well as Beatrix's, for that particular text to be erased. Larkin had learned all of that when she'd solved Bonnie Cooper's murder back in February—but she decided to take Jay's advice and not reveal everything she knew. Better to let her previous mysteries remain mysteries. Better to remain a mystery herself, for as long as possible, so Jay couldn't counter her moves before she had a chance to play them.

"So what's the answer?" Larkin asked. "How do you get your hands on potassium cyanide, when you can't go buy it from your local apothecary?"

"Who says you can't?" Jay asked, in return. "You have to adjust your definitions of *local* and *apothecary*, of course." He looked at Larkin. "The answer is the same as it always was."

Larkin thought, carefully, of all the ways somebody could get their hands on an illegal substance. Then she understood. *Same as it always was.* Jay didn't want her to think about how the murderer had gotten the poison. He wanted her to think about what the murderer had given in return.

"Money," Larkin said. "The answer is money."

"A lot of money," Jay corrected. "Which means it's time to stop thinking about *how* and start thinking about *whom.*"

CHAPTER 8

"We can figure this out together," Larkin said. She and Ed were seated on their bench, watching cumulonimbus accumulate. "Who has money?"

"Who has the means, you mean?" Ed said. "And is mean enough to do it."

"We can eliminate our former Juliet," Larkin said. "Even though she probably hates us for firing her—"

"Even though she got caught *in flagrante*—"

"And would love to see the production go down in flames." Larkin took a bite of her apple and set up her next serve. "But Amelia Jorgensen is a 21-year-old from Waterloo with exactly two assets."

"Unbruised youth and unstuffed brain," Ed said, quoting Friar Laurence. Larkin was hoping he'd make that choice, instead of swinging at *A Chorus Line*. Wordplay was their foreplay, after all—and if they could predict each other's responses, even better. "Manny could have loaned her the money," Ed suggested, continuing the game. "And for his payback, he could have taken—"

"A pound of flesh?" Larkin said. "I don't think we can make that joke, since Manny's actually Jewish."

"Really?" Ed asked.

"Yeah," Larkin said. "Clarissa isn't, though." Rebecca had told her, one night, that she didn't know which of her family's value systems to follow. "Should I make art, or money?" Rebecca had asked—and that gave Larkin both a clue and an idea.

"How much money does Manny stand to lose if he gets divorced?"

"What do you mean?"

"Any assets in that family have to come from Clarissa's side," Larkin said, taking a bite of her definitely-not-poisoned ham-and-cheese sandwich. It tasted like the plastic it had been wrapped in. "The Bankshaw brokerage."

"The Bankshavian brokerage," Ed quipped. Larkin could have predicted that response, too—but she didn't mind. Jay had been unpredictable, whispering "wrong move" into her ear, forcing her to ask him for the right one. If Ed had known about the Hamlet plan—and he should have known about the Hamlet plan—he would have said "wrong play," re-making the joke they had made the other night, pulling them into collaboration instead of pushing them into competition. That was how they worked, the two of them. The best moves were the ones they both saw coming.

"And the Bankshaws know everybody," Larkin said. "I think that was how Manny originally got hired as Artistic Director, like, ten years ago." She was still working out the network of Creative Corridor business associates. Larkin was pretty sure she had been hired to replace Manny because a baritone soloist had watched her solve a murder and save a production of Beethoven's Ninth Symphony.

The baritone had introduced her to his husband, an engineer turned entrepreneur turned investor, and then the two of them had introduced her to Sahil.

"Manny could have gotten hired on his own merits," Ed said. "That's usually how it works."

"That's never how it works," Larkin said, laughing, watching a tiny piece of ham fly out of her mouth. "Do you think I got hired for my merits?"

"Yes," Ed said. "I know exactly why Sahil hired you."

"Were you in the meeting or something?"

"No," Ed said, kissing her. "I just know *you*." He also knew it was time to change the subject. "Have you seen what Clarissa's brother's been up to?"

"Is that Freddie Jr.?" Larkin asked.

Ed nodded. "He's the one who created that roboadvisor app. There was something in the news, right before we left—" He looked at his sandwich, trying to decide if it was worth another bite. "Something about the algorithm and the way it gives financial advice."

"I haven't seen any news in, like, four weeks," Larkin said. "Plus, I get all of my finance advice from Anni."

"Who is only part robot," Ed said, smiling.

"The loveable kind," Larkin said, smiling back. They both liked Anni. "Not the kind that is going to destroy the world."

"The Bankshaws, on the other hand—" Ed's smile faded. "How involved do you think Clarissa is with all of that?"

Larkin shrugged. "I don't think she's doing roboadvisor algorithms. Rebecca told me that her mother doesn't have a job."

"Homemaking counts as a job," Ed said, "although I don't think Clarissa spends a lot of time scrubbing toilets or wiping dishes."

"Right," Larkin said. She wasn't quite sure what Clarissa Bankshaw Morris did all day, but she was pretty sure it didn't involve kitchen patrol or latrine duty. "Which makes the alimony question kind of interesting. If Clarissa doesn't have any current income—"

"Then Manny might not be able to claim any of her future income." Ed finished her sentence. Then he passed her the last bite of his sandwich.

"Plus, he's the one at fault," Larkin said. She wished she had a working phone so she could text Anni and ask about the financial intricacies of the Bankshaw-Morris situation. Maybe Manny would be entitled to some of the Bankshaw family money after a divorce, even after adultery. "But it wouldn't make sense for him to murder Tyler or try to murder Farah."

"You know her family has money," Ed said. "Farah Emerson's. Both sides. Loaded."

"Interesting," Larkin said. Everything kept coming back to Farah. Their Juliet. The sun around which the entire production circled. The gun that would have to go off. "But why would she murder Tyler, and why would she try to murder herself?"

She could hear Jay's voice, between her ears. *To take herself off the suspect list.*

"Well," Ed said, "she wouldn't have done it because she wanted a better scene partner. We've been working with Caleb all morning, and you are going to be lucky to get a functional Romeo by final dress."

Larkin knew, without having to ask, who was on the other half of Ed's *we*. Portia Breedlove, the woman who was everything Larkin wasn't. She also knew—deep within the part of her that was still trying to become her Best Self—that none of this mattered. Portia and Ed worked well together. If she got in the way of that—if she did anything to prevent Ed from trying to become his Best Self—she might as well end things with Ed right now.

He'd make a joke about how, if he had known, he would have eaten that last bite of his sandwich himself.

He'd make a pun on *Shakespeare* and *breakup*.

He'd make her smile, and that would make it all right, and Larkin would feel like she'd made another wrong move.

Ed was, as Claire often said, a keeper.

So Larkin kept quiet—which was how she heard the sound, amplified by the kicking of the wind and the cradle of the lake, of a smartphone receiving a series of notifications. Beatrix, assumedly, although Beatrix usually kept her phone on silent—and Beatrix was approaching them from an entirely different direction.

"We're going to hold Caleb and Farah's afternoon scene work in the Equity cabin," Beatrix called out, her sleek black hair blowing into her face and catching itself in her horn-rimmed glasses. "There's going to be a storm."

———

For the first time since arriving on the Summer Shakespeare campsite, Larkin felt cold. She had seen the Equity cabin when Sahil gave his sales-job tour; she had not been inside since, and was unprepared for the air conditioning. Equity actors were entitled, thanks to union rules, to a long list of creature comforts—which meant that their bunks had been provided with real mattresses, not to mention sheets and blankets and pillows. Their windows had screens and curtains. There was a dorm-sized refrigerator and an enormous microwave, and cabinets filled with cups and cutlery. The Equity actors also had indoor plumbing—a kitchen sink in the main room, and a toilet, sink, and shower behind a closet-sized door.

Farah had loaned Larkin a sweater. Portia had brought her own. "I think we should put Farah on the top bunk and Caleb by the ladder, don't you agree?" The Equity actors got bunks with ladders. Farah's sweater contained more natural fibers than Larkin's entire outfit. "Yes," she said, letting Portia set the scene. "That's probably the best way of doing this."

They didn't need the bunk, of course. If it had been just Larkin in charge of the rehearsal, she would have had Farah and Caleb rehearse the balcony scene sitting cross-legged on the floor. Looking at each other. Hooking their hands together. Pulling the truth out one line at a time.

But Portia was also in the cabin, and Ed, and they wanted to add music and movement to truth, and even though Larkin could have argued that Caleb wasn't ready for anything more complicated than Shakespeare's text, she decided to let them do their work. A Romeo who lacked precision was better than a Romeo who lacked confidence, and Caleb had already come too far to be asked to go backwards.

Farah was carrying them both, from her perch on the upper bunk. She had taken off her shoes, and the careful placement of her bare feet on the top rung of the ladder was enough to turn her into the fourteen-year-old Juliet. The bunk into the balcony. The chilly cabin into an Italian summer night.

"But soft," Caleb said, as if he couldn't believe it himself. "What light, through yonder window breaks."

A flash of lightning, diffused through the voile curtains. Larkin counted the seconds until the thunder-clap. Caleb continued. "It is the east, and Juliet is the sun. Arise, fair sun, and—*line*."

Camryn should have been there, to read from the prompt book, but she had been given the equally important task of stuffing the gift bags for Preview Night. All of the guests would go home with brand-new reusable water bottles, stamped with the logos of the biggest sponsors. Delicate paper fans, printed with Elizabethan-era paintings. A pop socket for each of their phones, shaped like William Shakespeare's head.

Everyone else in the cabin knew the line. Portia provided it. "Arise, fair sun, and kill the envious moon." Her voice was beautiful, though she spoke a dancer's truth instead of an actor's. Portia kept the pentameter intact, emphasizing *kill* instead of *moon*.

"Who is already sick and pale with grief," Caleb continued, picking up his pace to prove he knew it, "that thou her maid art far more fair than she."

"*Art far*," Ed said, turning the sounds into music. "We are not an aardvark."

Caleb looked to Larkin. He didn't need Ed and Portia, conducting and choreographing his every move. He needed direction.

So Larkin gave it.

"You already know what I'm going to ask," she said, smiling.

"Yeah," Caleb said, smiling back. He did know—which meant he knew what to do next.

"What does Romeo want?" Caleb asked, addressing the entire room. Then he shifted his weight onto the backs of his feet, as if he were looking up a two-story building instead of a bunkbed. He smiled at Farah. She held up her phone—a *fully-charged phone*, the Equity cabin had *electrical outlets*—and opened an app that flickered like a burning candle.

"But soft," Caleb said, again. This time he was Romeo,

wanting nothing more than to see Juliet's face. "What light through yonder window breaks? It is the east, and Juliet is the sun."

Larkin watched the scene. Caleb, doing the work. Farah, helping him. Romeo and Juliet, discovering each other for the first time. Portia, absorbed in the story. Ed, watching Larkin. He'd seen everything she'd done, over the past four weeks, to get to the point where she could get this kind of work out of Caleb by *asking him to ask himself a question.*

Ed wrote something in his palm-sized notebook. He tore out the page and passed it to Larkin.

This is why Sahil hired you.

This is why you don't have to worry about keeping your job.

CHAPTER 9

Everyone knew that final dress rehearsals were supposed to be dreadful. It was another one of the many superstitions that stitched theater companies together during what would otherwise be fraying days. *Bad final dress, good opening night.* Some people even believed that an unsuccessful dress rehearsal meant a successful run, three full weeks of sold-out shows and standing Os. Caleb, fresh off his success in the Equity cabin, was leading the college-aged cast members in a chant: "Bad final dress! Bad final dress!"

The Equity actors, who were experienced enough to at least pretend they didn't believe in superstition, were already working. Stretching, vocalizing, drinking individually wrapped bottles of coconut water. Preparing, as Konstantin Stanislavski once wrote. Building the empty space, as Peter Brooks had put it, so they could fill it with Shakespeare's words.

Larkin had very little to do to prepare. The final dress rehearsal was completely out of her control; Velvet and Camryn, as stage manager and assistant stage manager, would run the show. Final Dress was an opportunity to see what had been created. It was often viewed as a last chance to correct what might go wrong.

The first thing that had gone wrong was, of course, the weather. The non-Equity cast had spent part of their dinner break wiping down the injection-molded seats that thronged the amphitheater, just as they would be expected to do if it rained before a real performance. Their audience could not be asked to sit in puddles; the Equity cast could not be asked to give up their hour-long dinner. Larkin had grabbed a towel and joined in, wiping everything off just in time for it to start raining again.

Now Larkin sat underneath an umbrella, smelling the air as it wrung out its water. Hearing the bells that would bring the audience to their seats. If this were a real performance, Beatrix would be having some kind of secret text conversation with Sahil about the pros and cons of canceling. Whether there were enough seats at future performances to accommodate everyone who could be rescheduled; enough money to compensate those who would only be reimbursed. But it was only a final dress rehearsal, and final dress rehearsals were supposed to be dreadful. Everybody knew that.

Not that Larkin had anything to dread. She had Ed's note in her pocket, she had an understudy who was no longer underprepared, and she had—

"You haven't solved it yet, have you."

That was Jay. He had no umbrella, so Larkin was obliged to share hers. She didn't have to wonder if he'd planned it that way.

"Sorry," Larkin said. "Too busy saving the show."

"It's not saved until we know how Tyler died," Jay said.

"Potassium cyanide," Larkin said. "Just like the real Romeo."

"Is that what you're going to say at tomorrow's Previews?" The lights went down. The pre-recorded announcement began. *Thank you for coming. Thirty years of history. Two intermissions. Vendors. Donations. Volunteering. We'd tell you to silence your phones, but you're in one of the few places in Iowa that doesn't have cell service—so we'll just tell you to sit back, relax, and enjoy the show.*

"I hate that announcement," Larkin said. "When theater's done correctly, you're on the edge of your seat."

"Solve the murder," Jay said, "and I'll let you record a new one. You can exchange one cliché for another."

"Wrong move," Larkin said. "You don't get to *let me* do anything."

"I don't know," Jay said. "I've got you thinking about the murder again."

Larkin opened her backpack, took out her enormous floppy hat, and pushed it firmly onto her head. Then she closed her umbrella. Let Jay get wet, if he wanted to. He should have prepared for this.

"I choose my own thoughts," she said, "and right now I choose to think about the dress rehearsal." She took out her yellow legal pad and pulled it close enough to her body so that her hat could protect it from the rain. "You may sit here if you like, but don't expect my attention."

A small part of Larkin wanted to look at Jay, to see if she had impressed him—but her Best Self kept her eyes and her thoughts focused on the stage. *The which, if you with patient ears attend,* said the prologist—Caleb's former role, now filled by a supernumerary with a scroll—*what here shall miss, our toil shall strive to mend.*

That was the purpose of the final dress rehearsal, after all.

Not to fulfill a superstition, but to reveal that which had been shaped by toil and patience. To strive, to listen, to mend. To make art, which was never easy. To prepare for a Festival.

———

In the end it all went very well. So well that Larkin could feel her cast's anxiety, as she gathered them on the stage for their final notes. Some of them weren't confident in their ability to recreate what had just been created. Others were guarding themselves against any last-minute criticism. Larkin had been in those kinds of productions before; the ones where everything went so close to perfect that it was unbearable to hear the list of imperfections.

The worst part was that none of them knew what to expect. They'd never done Summer Shakespeare with Larkin Day before. They didn't know if she would be the kind of director who would keep them up all night, working and reworking missed cues. She could also be the kind of director who sent them straight to bed, telling them to check the callboard the next morning, warning them to prepare for a busy day, making it impossible for them to sleep.

Larkin had already decided to be a different kind of director. She knew what her cast wanted, and she knew they wouldn't be able to give the performance she wanted until they got it.

"That was exceptional work," Larkin said. "You know that, and you know I know that, and you know that I know you can do the same thing tomorrow." She smiled. "Not the *same,* same thing. That's mathematically impossible, as my friend Anni Morgan would say." Larkin saw Ed, at the corner of the stage, watching her be her Best Self. "But you can create something equally exceptional, if you give it your full attention. Just like you did tonight."

They waited. This was not what they wanted, not yet. All of those people seated on the stage, all of those faces she'd come to know so intimately over the past four weeks—they all wanted to be *set at ease*. They wanted to release the tension they'd been carrying, collectively, for the past four hours. They wanted it even more than they wanted to be told they'd done well, because they knew they'd done well. They didn't know if they would be given the rest they'd earned.

"That's all I'm going to say," Larkin said. "Now stand up."

They stood. Some of them guessed what was coming, and relaxed before Larkin asked them to.

"Arms over your head," Larkin said. She didn't have Portia's Alexander training, but it didn't matter. They wanted her, right now, more than they wanted Portia. Larkin Day was the only person who could set them free. "Shake, shake, shake, shake, shake, shake, shake, and *drop*."

Larkin folded over, knees bent, her fingertips brushing her toes. One of the college students misunderstood her direction and flopped to the ground. Everyone laughed. "Perfect," Larkin said. "Let your body go however it wants. There are no rules. I'm going to shake out my left leg, if you want to join me."

They did. They shook, shook, shook, shook, shook, shook, shook and dropped. They laughed. They swiveled their necks, their waists, their wrists, and their ankles. They stretched, forwards and backwards, until they each found their center.

Then they held hands. "I don't want to give you a bunch of notes that are just going to make you all nervous," Larkin said. "At this point you either know your part or you don't, and if you don't, you know what you need to do on your own. If you need any help, you know where to find me."

That was all she could do. Her role as Artistic Director was effectively over, not counting the speech she had to give at Preview Night—so she stepped out of the circle, Caleb and Farah clasping their hands to fill her gap.

"Goodnight, everybody," Larkin said.

She exited stage right.

She exited the amphitheater.

She walked the muddy path back to her cabin, her flashlight beam bouncing a few steps ahead of her. She tucked the light under her arm as she opened the cabin door, the beam revealing what was on the floor before she registered it.

A body, between the bunkbeds.

Face up, limbs splayed, bloodstained.

Juliet's dagger—the real one—embedded between the breasts.

Larkin shook, and then she dropped. Her flashlight illuminated the note, resting against the fingers of the corpse's left hand:

I did it. I wanted to play Juliet. I'm sorry.

It was Amelia Jorgensen.

CHAPTER 10

"I t is unfortunate," Larkin said, holding her glass of wine without sipping from it, "but at least it's solved."

The Cedar Rapids businessman, who had already swapped his empty glass for a fresh one, nodded enthusiastically. "And the show will go on!"

"The show *must* go on," Larkin corrected. He smiled. He loved her, this man she didn't know who had either made a bunch of money in the past or was likely to make a bunch of money in the future. He was part of the theater, this mysterious world with its actors and its music and its murder-suicides, for one intoxicating night. He almost knew the right thing to say.

Larkin had known what to say even before Sahil had told her. The words *murder* and *poison*, *dagger* and *suicide*, had been eliminated from her vocabulary as soon as she gave her second statement to the police. Larkin could say *unfortunate*. Larkin could say *unexpected*. Larkin could even say *tragic*, if she wanted—but the word she really needed to say, as often as possible, was *resolved*.

"You can say *solved*, if you want," Sahil had said. "If it would help your brand."

Larkin had wanted to point out that nobody had solved anything, not yet—but she could see the relief in Sahil's face and the warning in Jay's. So Larkin said nothing, agreed to everything, and six hours later stood in the center of a catered reception, watching the servers circle the crowd.

She was wearing an evening gown that had been purchased that afternoon, complete with shoes that glittered and undergarments that flattered. Stanley had taken her measurements, driven into Coralville, and charged the entire outfit to the Summer Shakespeare account. The dress she had bought out-of-pocket, at the beginning of the summer, still hung in its bag on the back of her bunk. It was understood, even before Sahil told her, that she and Ed and Rebecca and Beatrix would all need to find other places to live; that they would not be allowed back into the cabin where Amelia Jorgensen had died. Their belongings would be returned to them at some future date. Amelia's parents had been contacted. Tyler's parents would be informed. Everything was being taken care of—and Larkin was taking care of each and every guest who approached her, everyone wanting to see the Artistic Director who had solved the mystery.

"I've been to a dozen Preview Nights," one of them said, "but nothing like this."

"Nothing like this," Larkin said. It was an old theater trick, repeating what the other person had just said. It made them feel validated. It kept them talking. It kept Larkin from accidentally speaking the truth.

His second wife was giddy with her third glass of Champagne. "Who did your hair? You look amazing."

"I do look amazing," Larkin said. "You can thank our costume designer for that. He's over there."

She gestured towards Stanley, who was standing with Susan. Larkin had asked, while Stanley was manning the curling iron, if he and his wife would be able to resolve their own problems.

"Su and I have been married for forty-two years," Stanley had said. "Everything we do has already been resolved. We just go through this little dance, every once in a while, when we disagree on something. I don't even remember what it was, this time." He released a wave of Larkin's hair and pinned it into place. "We both hate the dance—Su said, the other day, *Stan, dahling, I hate the dahnce*—but it's got a bunch of steps, and it ends with the two of us cheek-to-cheek again, so we just gotta wait it out."

"Why can't you skip the steps, then?" Larkin had asked, as Stanley switched from her hair to her makeup.

"Because we don't know how," Stanley had said. "I'm hoping we'll figure it out in the next forty-two years."

Now Larkin watched SuStan share a plate of canapes. "Go say hello," she told the older businessman and his younger wife. "Susan and Stanley Levenstein. They'd love to meet you." The two Preview Night guests, delighted to receive Larkin Day's direction, toddled and tottered away. Larkin saw the look Susan gave Stanley, neither of them even needing to turn their heads. She saw Stanley grin. The two of them greeted the couple, the dog extending his paw and the pony shaking her mane. Agreeable, agreed upon, agreed anon. Larkin wished Ed was there, to watch Susan and Stanley celebrate forty-two years of marriage, but Ed was busy warming up the musicians. There would be viols and bassoons, recorders and sackbuts, as soon as the crowd got drunk enough to stop making profitable conversation.

One more round of drinks ought to do it, Larkin thought. Then—*I'm thinking like Jay.*

She looked around, knowing Jay Malhotra was somewhere in the mix, wondering when he would make his appearance. After Larkin had discovered Amelia's body, she'd had to walk from her cabin back to the amphitheater, to find someone who could help. Someone who could get in touch with the outside world. Someone who could confirm Amelia was dead.

Ed, Beatrix, and Jay.

Ed had held her hand. Beatrix had used her phone. Jay had examined the position of the dagger and the note between Amelia's fingers.

"It does look like a suicide," he said—and then he'd looked at Larkin.

She knew.

He knew.

Which meant she'd spent the entire evening waiting for Jay to come up behind her and whisper in her ear. *We both know it isn't resolved,* he would say. *We both know Amelia Jorgensen was murdered.*

But Jay Malhotra was unpredictable—and when Larkin finally spotted him, she saw something she hadn't been anticipating.

Jay, next to his parents.

Beatrix, in a cocktail dress that looked even more expensive than Larkin's gown, on his arm.

The two of them were almost unrecognizable. Jay looked subdued, a man paying his dues to his family, the angel and the devil snuffed off both his shoulders. Beatrix had removed her glasses and teased her hair. She'd put on lipstick and heels. She wore a tiny diamond ring and stood in a circle of confidence—something to do with money, something to do with matrimony, and nothing to do with love.

"Beatrix and Jay," Ed said. He had been the one to come up behind Larkin. He had been the one to whisper. "I wondered when they were going to make their announcement."

"You knew?" Larkin wasn't used to being the last person to figure something out.

"No," Ed said, "but I guessed." He squeezed Larkin's hand. "You see, my dear Watson, you have to ask yourself why Beatrix was hired."

"She and Jay are both from Chicago," Larkin said. "They must have known each other." Something about this didn't make sense. "Wait, are you saying that Sahil hired his son's girlfriend?"

"No," Ed said. "I'm saying that Sahil hired Beatrix so that he could evaluate her for a potential merger."

"So Beatrix and Jay weren't, like, boyfriend-girlfriend."

"No."

"But now they're fiancé-fiancée."

"Yes."

"And Beatrix's family must have, like, *a ton of money.*"

"Nope," Ed said. "The Malhotras provide the property. The Yangs provide the intellectual property. Guess what Beatrix does when she's not assistant-company-managing Shakespeare festivals?"

"What?"

"No," Ed said. "For real. *Guess.*"

Larkin watched Beatrix, who was no longer displaying her ring. Instead, she was showing off her phone—and putting on her horn-rimmed glasses.

"Beatrix makes glasses that have tiny Wi-Fi routers in

them," Larkin said, "so you can get internet no matter where you go."

"You're so close," Ed said. "In fact, I'd say you were extremely hot." He appraised and then gazed at Larkin. "Pun intended."

"Thank our costume designer," Larkin said.

"Stan only gilded the lily," Ed said. "You were the one who blossomed."

He kissed her, quietly and privately, at the very edge of her smile. "I'll mess up that makeup job later," he said. "Now guess again."

"Something to do with internet."

"Yes."

"Something to do with why Beatrix has internet and we don't."

"Yes."

"A product she's testing that she wants Sahil to invest in."

"Her father is the one who wants Sahil to invest," Ed said, "but I'll allow that as a *yes*."

"How do you know all of this?" Larkin asked. "No, wait, I know the answer. You and Beatrix talked it all over at 5 a.m., while you were lifting weights and she was testing her secret internet device."

"You're such a good detective," Ed said. "I almost wish you still had a murder to solve." A viol began to tune; the crowd began to quiet. Larkin watched Ed watching her. He knew, or at least he suspected, what she knew—that there was, in fact, another murder to solve. He also knew something she didn't.

"I'll tell you mine if you tell me yours," she whispered.

"Beatrix Yang's father is testing a solar-powered Wi-Fi router," Ed said.

"Amelia Jorgensen didn't commit suicide," Larkin said.

The jangle of Elizabethan instrumental music snagged at the sparkle of the night. Period instruments were never quite as romantic as people expected, especially since the Romantic period wouldn't begin for another 250 years. A few people attempted to check their phones, before they remembered why they couldn't. The crowd shifted their feet, applauded politely, and parted, drunk and unaware, as Portia pushed her way toward Ed and Larkin.

"We have a problem," she said. "Farah is gone."

CHAPTER 11

The three of them—Larkin, Ed, and Portia—stood by Farah's former bunk in the Equity cabin. The sheets had been stripped, the blankets neatly folded. A note, written in a careful hand, placed on top of the pillow:

I am tendering my resignation effective immediately.

You may contact my agent about any financial or contractual concerns.

Best,

Farah Emerson

"We have a performance in thirty minutes," Larkin said. She looked carefully at Portia. She looked even more carefully at Ed. Neither of them had asked, on the walk over to the Equity cabin, whether Farah might have been murdered. Neither of them had suggested checking any other location. Portia had led them directly towards Farah's bunk as if she had already known what they would find.

Larkin would interrogate them later. Both of them, separately and then together.

Right now, she had a show to save.

"Portia," Larkin said, "you're playing Juliet."

"We have an understudy—"

"Who isn't prepared for this," Larkin said. "You are."

She watched Portia's eyes narrow. She watched Portia's weight rise, her diaphragm expanding, her body leaning into the balls of her feet. Fight-or-flight. Larkin was right.

"You don't think we did this on purpose—"

"It doesn't matter what I think," Larkin said. She was very interested in who was on the other half of Portia's *we*. Was it Portia-and-Farah, or Portia-and-Ed? "What I know," Larkin continued, looking first at her boyfriend and then at her choreographer, "is that you know the part."

"I know the blocking," Portia said. "I know the dance. I do not know the text."

"You know it well enough," Larkin said. "Better than the understudy."

"I'll go up on my lines," Portia said. "You'll need to give me something to wear, an earbud or something, so Camryn can prompt me."

"No," Larkin said. Whatever Portia and the other half of her *we* had planned, it had not included her being asked to take on the role of Juliet—which was an interesting piece of information, but irrelevant to the current problem. "Camryn will not be told. Velvet will not be told. Sahil will not be told. The actors will not be told. Nobody will know that you are playing Juliet until you walk onstage in act 1, scene 3."

"We have to tell somebody," Ed said.

"We do not," Larkin said, "and we will not. If we tell anybody, then Preview Night gets canceled. If we start the show, and then Portia enters in Juliet's costume and begins reciting Juliet's lines, Velvet and Camryn will keep the show running."

"How do you know that?" Portia asked.

"Because they work in community theater," Larkin said, "and they've seen worse." Community theater stage managers were trained to keep the show running no matter what happened. No matter who missed their cue, no matter which part of the set fell over, no matter who walked onstage wearing whose costume. No matter how many Juliets died or disappeared.

"You know there are union rules," Ed said. "Both the actors' union and the dancers' union."

"I will, personally, eat any fines that need to be paid to any unions," Larkin said. "I will also, personally, reimburse the Festival for the destruction of this script." She took Farah's copy of *Romeo and Juliet* off the bunkbed. Juliet's lines had been tidily highlighted, in pink. "Ed," she said, "you are going to spend the next thirty minutes gluing Juliet's lines onto the backs of as many of those Elizabethan paper fans as you can find. Portia, you're going to carry a fan whenever you're onstage." She looked at her co-conspirators. "Do we all understand what is going to happen?"

Portia nodded, anxiously. Ed nodded, appreciatively. He knew. She knew. All three of them knew, without speaking, that Portia and Ed still knew something Larkin didn't—and Larkin didn't care.

"Get to work," she said, sweeping herself and her evening gown out of the Equity cabin. "I've got to go give a speech."

———

"Friends, Romans, countrymen," Larkin said, with a smile, giving the assembled audience an opportunity to laugh. "Wait—is that the play we're doing tonight?"

"That's *Julius Caesar*," came a voice from the second row.

"Right," Larkin said, directing just enough attention towards her heckler to ensure that he would make a sizable donation. "This gentleman knows his Shakespeare!" Then she took a few steps downstage left. Stanley had given her a lavalier mic, tucked gently into her décolletage, so she wouldn't have to carry a microphone. "The truth is that many of us know the stories Shakespeare told, even before we were old enough to realize we knew them."

She pointed both her eyes and her fingers towards the tenth row. "You, sir, in the seersucker." Larkin picked him because he'd been leering at her. "You're in love with a beautiful maiden, but before you can marry her, you have to prove yourself worthy by passing a simple test. You can open one of three boxes—a glittering gold box, a shimmering silver box, or a plain box made of lead. Which do you choose?"

"The lead one," the man said, without hesitation. "That's what Indiana Jones would do."

"It's also what Shakespeare did," Larkin said, "right after giving us the phrase *all that glitters is not gold.*" She smiled at her audience. "I'll give two comp tickets to the first person who can name the play I just referenced."

"*The Merchant of Venice!*" A voice, from the back row. It sounded like Ben, the baritone soloist who had watched Larkin solve her first murder and helped her get her current job. She'd wondered when he and his engineer-entrepreneur-investor husband Mitchell would arrive. "Well done," Larkin said. "Talk to the box office at intermission, and we'll get those tickets taken care of." She took a step towards center and softened her gaze to take in what was quickly becoming an adoring audience. "They get to see *Romeo and Juliet* twice. Does it matter that they already know the ending? Does it matter that you do?"

"No!" said her second-row heckler. This time Larkin ignored him.

"I think it does," she said. She gave the audience just enough time to ask themselves why she'd said that. Then she gave them her answer. "We come to these stories not because we want something new, but because we want something very, very old. Something primal. A truth so central to the human experience that we keep turning away from it. Our storytellers are the ones who turn our faces back, towards the fire. Towards the light. Towards the people we could become if we could pay attention."

Larkin nodded towards the booth, giving her cue to Velvet. The houselights dimmed; the spotlight surrounded her.

"That's why this evening is so important. After three years of unprecedented hiatus, we're finally able to produce Shakespeare again. To ask for your attention— and earn it." The light was too bright for Larkin to see anybody's faces. She assumed Sahil was smiling. She assumed Jay was smirking. It didn't matter. She would get what she wanted. They all would. "We've worked very hard on this production of *Romeo and Juliet*, and we've had our own tragedy to navigate," Larkin continued. "But there have been many tragedies, for many people, since we last took the stage together—and because of that we have a responsibility. To you. To Iowa, and the Creative Corridor. To the story we're about to share."

There was only one way her speech could end.

"We'll have a moment of silence," Larkin said, "and then we'll begin."

———

When Romeo first saw Juliet, he gasped. Caleb's reaction was so earnest, so honest, so *completely bewildered* that Larkin wished she could secretly switch cast members more often. The Nurse and Lady Capulet, both old Equity hands, had dispatched their previous scene with Portia without a lapse, playing it for laughs, the Nurse's surprise at Portia's appearance pulled inward and then pushed outward, towards the audience. *You see?* she seemed to say. *Even I don't know who this girl's become!*

But Caleb, who had never expected to become Romeo, was not expecting this Juliet. The audience understood the moment in a way they, too, were not expecting—a glance, between two people, changing everything. Larkin had staged the moment to allow Romeo to take one last look at the fair Rosalind before switching his attention and his allegiance to Juliet, but Caleb forgot—and the actress playing Rosalind, denied her one moment of interaction with the story, backed away with such acceptance that the audience understood, immediately, *what Romeo wanted.*

"What lady is that?" Caleb asked.

It was a real question—and it was asked in anger.

As the scene progressed, the audience got a new understanding of *who Romeo was*. The actor who had actively rooted for a bad final dress rehearsal became the lover who was actively routing the Capulets towards disaster. It was unclear, during the balcony scene, whether Romeo meant a single thing he said. It was clear that Caleb did not want to marry Juliet, even though Portia kept trying to carry the line in a direction that suggested she still wanted to marry Romeo. When the two of them argued, in bed, over whether they had heard the lark or the nightingale, it was a true argument—and one that nearly everybody in the theater had personally experienced. *Stay,* Juliet asked. *No,* Romeo answered.

It stopped being a story of star-crossed lovers. It became, instead, a story of woe—more woe, in Juliet and her Romeo, than any of them had ever seen. The audience started crying as soon as Portia brought out her draught of belladonna. They knew, this time, that there was no need to suspend their belief. No need to hope that this would be the one production of *Romeo and Juliet* where the lovers were allowed to live. The false hope belonged solely to the teenage girl who had taken responsibility for the situation she had been manipulated into. The daughter who still hoped her family's feud could be reconciled. The wife who put herself to sleep, trusting that her husband would want her to wake up.

The play ended with another moment of silence.

Then the applause—hesitant, at first, as if it seemed inappropriate to break what had been created. Then faster, hands and feet rising, the audience releasing its shared tension. The cast and crew were as bewildered as Caleb had been. Nobody had expected what had just happened. Nobody had known what would happen next. They had survived it, together—which is what everyone always wanted, when they sat down to a performance of *Romeo and Juliet*.

To come out alive.

"I'd like to believe we'll get that same performance tomorrow night," Mitchell said, as the stars came out and the audience went home, "but I think we just got a once-in-a-lifetime experience."

"All theater is a once-in-a-lifetime experience," Ben said. He was still holding the Elizabethan paper fan that had been placed in his swag bag. Now he waved it in

Larkin's direction. "I love that you turned this cheap piece of junk into Juliet's fan. You are going to sell so many of these things at intermission. Was that Sahil's idea?"

"No," Larkin said. "It was mine."

"As was your decision to cast Portia Breedlove?" Mitchell, who was a member of the Summer Shakespeare Board, was well aware of the switch. "With, what, half-an-hour until curtain?"

"It was last-minute," Larkin said. "We decided to proceed with the evening without doing anything that might inadvertently compromise the Preview Night mission." She did not tell him who was on the other half of her *we*. She let him assume it was Sahil—who had just arrived, with Rupa and Jay and Beatrix, to join them.

"We're keeping her, right?" Mitchell asked. "After what she just did?"

"We may have to," Sahil said. Larkin could tell that he was not happy with what had just happened—neither the change of cast nor, she suspected, the change of interpretation—but he was having trouble reconciling his emotions with his bottom line. "Do you know how many people just told me this was the best Shakespeare performance they'd ever seen?"

"And I thought they'd done well the last time I saw it," Rupa said. Larkin could tell that Sahil's wife still believed that everything had been resolved. Tyler was poisoned, Amelia confessed, cyanide and suicide. The show had gone on. The show had gone even better than expected. Everything else was inconsequential.

Sahil was out for consequences. "What happened to—"

"Is Farah Emerson all right?" Jay interrupted, taking control of the situation before his father could lose it.

"Yes," Larkin said. "Farah let me know, right before the show began, that she would be unable to perform."

"So she's not—" Sahil began.

"No," Larkin interrupted, taking control of the sentence before Sahil could finish it.

"And she'll be able to perform tomorrow?" Jay asked.

"Yes," Larkin said, taking refuge in a technicality. "Farah Emerson will be able to perform the role of Juliet on Opening Night." Whether Farah would perform the role of Juliet was another question, and one that Larkin wouldn't be able to answer until she spoke to Farah in person. She didn't need to interrogate Ed and Portia anymore, which was good—but the conversation the three of them needed to have with Farah could still go badly. "I really should go congratulate the cast," Larkin said. "And the crew. They did amazing work tonight, and they deserve to hear it from me."

"And you deserve to hear it," Mitchell said, "from us."

"Thank you," Larkin said. She took her bow and made her exit, aware that Beatrix had been tasked to follow her. Aware that Jay had decided to follow her on his own, under the pretense of accompanying his fiancée. So she did exactly what she had said she was going to do. Larkin congratulated the cast. She congratulated the crew. She told them how well they'd done, to help Portia and each other through the performance. She told them that Sahil had said it was the best Shakespeare many of the audience members had ever seen.

"Where's Farah?" Caleb asked. He, like Sahil, was still angry with the way the evening had gone. Larkin could see the tension coiling itself around his wrists and knees, preventing him from accepting what they had just achieved. He stretched out his hands, searching for release, and Larkin watched his energy zip-zap-zop its way to Portia—who shifted her weight, opened her mouth, and then remembered that she wasn't supposed to answer.

"Farah let me know that she wouldn't be able to do the performance tonight," Larkin said, for the second time that evening. "She's fine," she said, looking directly at Portia. "I believe she's staying with some friends." Portia's left shoulder relaxed, and Larkin knew she'd guessed correctly.

"She'll be back tomorrow," Jay said, moving with confidence into the center of the circle. "I'm sure of it. We've already been told that Farah will be able to perform on Opening Night, after all." He winked at Larkin. He eyed Portia. "An excellent performance, Ms. Breedlove," Jay said. "I'll make sure my father knows just how involved you were with tonight's success."

Larkin still hadn't looked at Ed. She knew exactly where he was, in the room, and she knew that he knew that she was avoiding his eyes. Jay hadn't yet turned his attention towards Dr. Jackson, which meant that Larkin still had more information than he did.

So Larkin kept her secret—and her advantage. "Don't worry," she said, taking her place next to Jay. Giving him a smile. "We've got it all under control. Now congratulate Jay and Beatrix, everybody—because they just got engaged tonight!" Larkin beckoned Beatrix towards the center of the circle. "Come take a look at this ring, everybody," she said, holding up Beatrix's hand, letting the cast fill in the gaps, squeezing her way between them. Brushing Portia's arm, as she passed her. Taking Ed's. Leading them both offstage.

"I know you both know where Farah is," Larkin said. She looked at Portia. "I could trick you into telling me, but then you'd think I was an asshole, and I'd rather have you on my side." She looked at Ed, for the first time since leaving the Equity cabin. "I know you aren't going to tell me, otherwise you'd have told me already. You must have made a promise to Farah, to keep her location a secret, and I value your integrity, and I won't ask you any more questions, and I'm still going to find her."

"Of course you are," Ed said. "I never thought you wouldn't."

"I love you too," Larkin said. "And now the two of you are coming with me to Pratincola."

CHAPTER 12

They took Ed's car—Larkin and Ed up front, and Portia in the backseat. They couldn't have taken Larkin's car, even if they'd wanted to, because Larkin's car keys and house keys were still in the cabin where Amelia's body had been found.

But Larkin wanted Ed's car. Not just because Ed had kept his car keys, which weren't even keys at all but some kind of electronic fob, zipped in the inner pocket of his shorts. Not just because Ed was an exceptionally good driver.

Larkin wanted Ed's car because Ed's car was also a phone.

"Call Elliott Fox," Larkin said, as soon as they hit the highway.

Elliott didn't pick up right away, but Larkin wasn't expecting him to. He was staying in Anni's studio apartment until they bought their house, after all. It would take him a minute to do what he needed to do before he could answer a phone.

"Elliott," Larkin said, when they finally connected.

"Larkin," Elliott said. "You're in Ed's car."

"And you're in the hallway outside of Anni's apartment, because Anni's already gone to sleep."

"Well detected," Elliott said. "How can I help you?"

"Are the two of you free for lunch tomorrow?"

"Yes," Elliott said. "We're doing a house tour at eleven, but after that we're free."

"Noon at The Coffee Shop?"

"Can do," Elliott said. "May we expect both our director and our musical director?"

Larkin looked at Ed. "I'm not sure," she said. "It may depend on how the rest of the night goes."

"Then I hope it goes well," Elliott said. "Since you've only got about twelve minutes of it left."

The next call was to Josephine Day.

"Mom," Larkin said. "Sorry to wake you."

"If I hadn't accepted that giving birth to you would mean that someday you might wake me up at 11:53 p.m.," Larkin's mother said, "we wouldn't be having this conversation right now."

"You can go back to bed in a minute," Larkin said. "Everything's fine. I just need you to leave the door unlocked, okay? I don't have my keys, everything's fine, I just don't have them, and I'm going to be sleeping over tonight."

"Has someone else been murdered?"

Larkin wasn't sure how to answer this question. She was pretty sure Farah hadn't been murdered. She was less sure about Amelia. "Everything's fine," she said, for the third time. Then she offered the one piece of information that she knew would keep her mother from thinking about murders all night long. "Ed's going to sleep over too."

"Oh!" This delighted Larkin's mother, who loved Ed nearly as much as Larkin did. "I suppose I should say something about how I'll make up the couch for him, but we both know he's sleeping in your bedroom, and that's fine with me, that's absolutely fine, it's really fine, and maybe we can have pancakes tomorrow."

"Sounds good," Larkin said. Her mother was terrible at making pancakes, but she and Ed could handle an undercooked breakfast—assuming they could handle everything that still had to happen before morning.

"Is Ed there now?"

"Yes," Larkin said. "He's driving."

"Then drive safely," Josephine said, "and I'll see you both soon."

"Go back to sleep," Larkin said. "It could be a few hours."

"And everything's fine," Josephine said again.

"Everything's fine," Larkin repeated. "Turn here," she whispered to Ed. He'd been expecting this; the turn signal and brakes were activated before Larkin had the chance to finish her sentence. He'd known she would figure it out. She just needed to know whether he'd hoped she would.

"Your mother is a very relaxed woman," Portia said, from the backseat. Nobody had ever called Josephine Day *relaxed* before. Larkin wasn't sure her mother would appreciate the compliment. The former academic dean might employ it as a reason to become re-employed. "My mother would not have believed that everything was fine," Portia continued.

"My mother doesn't believe it either," Larkin said, "but she's always let me figure out my own problems."

"No wonder you became an amateur detective," Ed said, taking the next turn before Larkin asked him to. Crossing the bridge as they came to it. This wasn't their first investigation. It wasn't even their first argument. It could be, in both cases, their best one.

"I have one more call to make," Larkin said, directing her voice towards the dashboard. "Call Ben Blankenship."

Ben's baritone quickly filled the car. "Ed!" he said. "We were just talking about you. Farah's being the perfect houseguest, no trouble at all, she's looking at flights right now, we're all going to bed in a minute, I swear."

"Good to know," Ed said. He reached out and squeezed Larkin's hand. The night was going well—he knew it, she knew it—but there were still a few questions Larkin needed to ask, and a few things Ed might need to answer for.

"Would you like to talk to her?" Ben asked.

"Yes," Larkin said, as the car pulled to a stop in front of Ben and Mitchell's mansion. "In person. In about thirty seconds."

"Larkin!" Ben said. "I guess Mitchell wins the bet, then." The porch lights flicked on. "He thought you'd figure it out before midnight, and I thought it would take you at least until tomorrow morning."

"You underestimate her," Ed said.

"Well, come on in," Ben said, as Mitchell opened the front door. "I'll tell the robots to start the coffee."

CHAPTER 13

"You see, my dear Watson," Larkin said, returning Ed's ribbing as he put his arms around her waist, "you have to ask yourself why Ben and Mitchell weren't at the Preview Night reception."

Ed rubbed his nose against hers. "You would ask yourself that, wouldn't you."

"And you have to ask yourself why you and Portia weren't at all worried about Farah."

Ed brushed his lips against hers. "You could ask yourself that, couldn't you."

"And you have to ask—no, wait, I have to kiss you first."

"You should," Ed said, and they did, and then Larkin turned her face towards the fragrance of a freshly brewed espresso.

"Coffee for the lady," Ben said, "and I hope you always come into our home dressed like that." Larkin was still wearing the gown Stanley had bought for her. "It's like you're a completely different person."

"I'm the same Larkin Day I always was," Larkin said,

inhaling and then swallowing the contents of her demi-tasse. "It's just, like, all of the other stuff that was keeping me from becoming her is, like, going away." She wiped her mouth on the back of her hand, smearing her lipstick. "Anni said it better."

"Well, she's the writer," Ben said. "And now we have an actor, a director, a choreographer, a conductor, a host, and—what role do you play in this scene, love?"

Mitchell, wrapped in a silk kimono and matching slippers, sipped from his own tiny cup. "I'm the engineer."

"And here I was, waiting for you to say you were the money," Ben said, leading Larkin and Ed from the kitchen to the music room. "But he really did engineer all of it," he continued, seating them next to Portia and Farah. "Including the clue."

"See?" Larkin said, kissing Ed's cheek and leaving a red smear on his violet skin. "You have to ask why Mitchell knew that I had asked Portia to play Juliet with just thirty minutes to curtain."

"You played Juliet?" Farah asked.

Portia looked at her dancer's feet. "Not as well as you."

"She did wonderfully," Larkin said. "You all did." She kissed Ed's other cheek, so it would match. "You asked Mitchell to tip me off, didn't you."

"Of course not," Ed said. "I promised Farah I wouldn't do anything to reveal her location."

"And then he told me what he had promised," Mitchell said.

"And tomorrow I'm leaving for good," Farah said, "and I'm not telling any of you where."

She stood up—the most beautiful thing in the room, despite Larkin's evening gown and Mitchell's kimono and Ed's lipstick-stained cheek and the Bösendorfer grand piano with its nine extra keys and the jade vase with its fresh-cut flowers and the framed Playbill of *Sunday in the Park with George* that had been signed by both Bernadette Peters and Mandy Patinkin—and put her phone in her pocket. "I'm going to the airport tomorrow morning. Right now, I'm going to bed. Ben, Mitchell, you've been excellent hosts. Larkin, it's been a pleasure working with you. Portia, I wish I could have seen you perform. Ed, well—" Farah smiled. "I should have known better than to trust you."

She turned, to make her exit—and Larkin quickly asked herself *what Farah wanted.*

"Hold, please," she said, in her best Artistic Director voice. Farah, Equity-trained, held.

"We're going to do this scene again," Larkin said. "This time, I want to know more about what you thought Ed would do for you. Did you really believe that he wouldn't tell me where you were?"

"I don't know," Farah said. "I suppose part of me did."

"And what did the other part of you want?"

Farah looked at her hands. She looked at the window. She looked at the unlit fireplace, and at Mitchell's decanter of single-malt scotch. "I can't say," she finally said. "I suppose—"

They waited. She had their attention, all of it.

"I suppose *this.*"

"Yes," Larkin said. "It's what you've wanted ever since you fake-stabbed yourself with the real dagger."

"Someone tried to kill me," Farah said, "and nobody cared."

"Come here," Larkin said, standing up and holding out her arms. Farah stepped forward and accepted the embrace. "I care. I've been trying to figure out, from the beginning, why you were the target. There's a yellow legal pad, which I don't have anymore, it's in my backpack in the cabin that they won't let us go into until they clean up all the blood, but there are at least two different pages on that legal pad that ask why someone tried to kill you."

"Someone tried to kill me," Farah said again, her face muffled by Larkin's shoulder. She was crying—really crying—and Larkin let her. "And I wanted to play Juliet, I really did. I loved it."

"I know," Larkin said. This next moment had to be played very carefully, to ensure that *what Larkin wanted* didn't get in the way of *what Farah wanted*—and to ensure that Larkin didn't inadvertently do *what the murderer wanted*.

What did the murderer want?

Larkin realized that she hadn't yet asked herself that question. She'd asked herself why the murderer might have done it, which was a different question. *Motive*—the reason the murderer became a murderer—was backward-facing. *Desire*—the situation the murderer was hoping to create, as quickly as possible—was the path forward.

So she turned around. "We all want Farah to play Juliet, right?"

Mitchell understood, immediately. "Yes," he said. "The Board was very enthusiastic about her casting."

Larkin nodded. Mitchell was on her side. Next up was Portia. "And we already know that we have at least one member of our company who is committed to keeping Farah safe."

"Two," Portia said. "I couldn't have done any of this without Ed."

"Right," Larkin said. "But Farah doesn't trust Ed right now, since Ed's the person who prevented her from getting on a plane." She kissed Ed a third time, her remaining lipstick sticking to his lips. "You have to ask, my dear Dr. Jackson, why you waited until the end of the day to drive Farah over to Ben and Mitchell's mansion."

"Eastern Iowa Airport closes at midnight," Ed said. "I drove Farah over while Stanley was doing your hair and makeup. Ben and Mitchell insisted on making her dinner before they left for Preview Night."

"So Farah was alone, in a house full of antiques and robots, with no Wi-Fi password and no access to a car," Larkin said.

"I gave her the Wi-Fi password," Ben said. "I'm not *evil*."

"But even if she had been able to book a ticket on the last flight out," Larkin said, "she wouldn't have been able to get to the airport."

"Correct," Ed said. He was delighted to have created the perfect plan. "Unlike Ben, I might have been a little bit evil."

"Couldn't she have taken a taxi?" Portia asked. She was unaware of the plan's perfection. Ed must not have told her. He must have known she'd tell Farah.

"Taxis have a terrible time finding this place," Ben said, "and don't get me started on Uber."

"And then Ed got Ben and Mitchell to bet on how long it would take for me to figure it out," Larkin continued, "ensuring Mitchell would engineer a way to get me here before Farah could take an early-morning flight."

"Correct again," Ed said.

"Which means that Farah is also correct," Larkin said, "not to trust Ed Jackson." Then she sat down, on the ottoman, so that she could look directly into Farah's golden eyes. "But here's the deal. Ed did all of this—*all of it*—so that you and I would be able to have this conversation, right now. Because he trusts me. Because he trusts that I can keep you safe—*me, of all the people in this room*—until we figure out who tried to kill you."

Larkin looked at the clock. It was 12:43 a.m..

"Here is what is going to happen," she said. "Farah, you're staying here tonight. Portia, you're staying with her. Ed, you're coming with me. We're all getting a lot of sleep, and then Ed and I are going to go have lunch with two of our best friends. One of them is the smartest person I know. The other one is the nerdiest person I've ever met."

"He used to have his own TV show," Ben said, as if that explained everything.

"The four of us are going to come up with a plan. It's probably going to involve something like making Farah wear a bracelet that tracks her location at all times, I'm not sure what the plan is yet, but there will be a way for me to always know where you are." She looked at Farah. Then she looked at the four other people in the room. "And to always know that one of us is with you."

"I'm sorry, Larkin," Mitchell said, "but I've read a few cozy mysteries in my day, and I have to ask the obvious question. What if one of us is the murderer?"

"I was hoping you'd ask," Larkin said, "because it's very easy to prove that nobody in this room wants Farah dead." She looked at each person in turn. "Portia wanted Farah to be in Chicago by now, or maybe Boston, but she didn't know that Ed would make it impossible for Farah to take a flight. Ed wanted Farah to stay in Pratincola long enough for me to figure it out, and Ben and Mitchell had money riding on how quickly I would put the pieces together."

"It wasn't money," Ben said. "Our bets are much more interesting."

"Either way," Larkin said. "We all want Farah to be alive."

"*Quod erat demonstrandum,*" Ed said.

"*Ça marche,*" Portia said.

"*O Freunde, nicht diese Töne!*" Ben said. "I know other languages too."

Larkin watched Farah's body language. The actor's hands had opened, relaxing, letting the tension flow from her fingers to the fibers of Ben and Mitchell's carpet. She almost had what she wanted. They both did.

"And we all want you to stay alive," Larkin finished, "so you can play Juliet on Opening Night."

What did the murderer want?

"All right," Farah said. "I believe you."

"Good," Larkin said. "And if anyone asks, we all believe the other story. The one where Amelia Jorgensen killed Tyler and then killed herself."

"Nobody who'd read any cozy mysteries would believe that story," Mitchell said. "Which means you have two murders and one attempted murder to solve."

"Shall we make another bet?" Ben asked.

"I don't care what you do," Larkin said, "as long as you keep Farah safe." She held out her hand; Ed took it. "We'll be back tomorrow."

CHAPTER 14

"Did you sleep all right?" Josephine asked, the next morning. She was seated at her usual spot at the kitchen table, eating one of the pancakes she had tried to make before Claire took over. Larkin watched her mother cut her way through the burned pancake crust—she was pretty sure pancakes weren't supposed to have crusts—into its oozing middle.

"We slept fine," Larkin said. She and Ed had arrived at the Day house a little after one in the morning. The two of them had showered, together, before sharing Larkin's bed. They hadn't done anything Larkin wouldn't have wanted to tell her mother about—in fact, Ed had already given her permission to share the conversation.

"This is the beginning of our dance," Larkin had said, her cheek against Ed's bare chest, thinking of what Stanley had told her. "The things we do right now, they're like the steps we're learning."

"The music we're composing," Ed said.

"The tunes that'll get stuck in our heads," Larkin said.

"I get it," Ed said. "We need to make sure they're good ones."

"The best ones," Larkin said, somewhere between happiness and sleep, "if we want to be our Best Selves."

Now she watched her mother and Claire carry out their respective tasks—cooking, caring, welcoming—as she and Ed sipped coffee and tea. A perfect pancake was placed in front of her. An aging dog nuzzled her ankles for a scrap of bacon. The man she loved rubbed the pad of his thumb against the back of her hand.

What did the murderer want?

"I need to go for a bike ride," Larkin said. "By myself. Is that okay?"

"It's hot out there," Claire said. "Take a water bottle."

"And a helmet!" Larkin's mother said.

"Yeah, I know," Larkin said. "And stay on the protected bike lanes." She loved her mother, and she loved Claire, and she was loving Ed more and more every day— but she needed to be alone. She hadn't been alone, not really, since the start of the Shakespeare Festival.

"Will you be all right?" she said, kissing Ed's forehead.

"Of course," Ed said. "I'll check in on Portia and Farah, see how they're surviving Ben and Mitchell's smarthome." He smiled at Larkin. "Pun intended."

"I'm pretty sure their coffee machine could in fact kill you if you gave it the wrong voice command," Larkin said, squeezing Ed's hand. They had all agreed, long ago, that they could make jokes about murder investigations.

"Did you say *ex-press-o*?" Claire said, in a robot voice. "I thought you said *ex-ter-mi-nate*."

"One of these days I want to see this house," Josephine said. "I've heard so much about it."

"You will," Larkin said, twitching her nose at her mother. "But right now I gotta clear my head and get ready to meet Anni and Elliott at The Coffee Shop for lunch." She put on her shoes and gave the golden retriever a head scritch. "This is another reason I'm glad I'm getting out of the barista industry. Live theater will be the last job to be replaced by robots."

"Theater," Josephine said, twitching her nose back, "and teachers."

"And detectives," Claire said. "So get going."

————

Larkin *got*—and as soon as she got outside, back into the unexpected familiarity of an Iowa summer, using muscles that had become stronger through four months of fitness classes and four weeks of walking around the Festival campground, she found her mind suddenly prepared to address her question.

"What does the murderer want?" Larkin said aloud.

Her first answers articulated themselves in cadence with her pedaling. Uphill, low gear, just inefficient enough to be frustrating. "The murderer wanted Tyler dead. The murderer wanted Amelia dead. The murderer may have wanted Farah dead. The murderer may still want Farah dead."

Then she crested, coasted, and let both her mind and her ride pick up speed.

Did the murderer want certain people to die—or was the murderer more interested in achieving a certain outcome? Did the murderer want to stop Tyler from existing, or did the murderer want to stop Tyler from playing Romeo, or did the murderer want to stop the entire show?

"What would happen if Tyler died?" Larkin asked, aloud, squeezing her brakes just enough to satisfy her mother's concerns about bike safety. "We'd cast the understudy," she said, signaling her turn with her left hand. "Which we did."

She began pedaling again. This path took her by the Pratincola Fitness Complex, where she had solved the murder of Bonnie Cooper. "Could Caleb have done it? Maybe. He could have poisoned Tyler, and he could have stabbed Amelia and made it look like a suicide. With a confession note. That would have gotten him off the hook."

The trouble was that Caleb hadn't really wanted to play Romeo—or maybe he had, Larkin had never met an actor who hadn't secretly wanted to play *all the parts*, but Caleb hadn't done any of the work. There were two kinds of understudies; the ones who had the entire role ready to go, just in case the lead woke up with a tickle in their throat, and the ones who told themselves that they still had time to learn the lines. Caleb had been in the latter camp, for as long as they'd been on the campsite. He wouldn't have given Tyler cyanide; he would have offered him acai berries and echinacea.

"Next question," Larkin said. "What would happen if Tyler stopped playing Romeo?"

This was almost the same question as the one she'd just asked—but not quite. "If Tyler stops playing Romeo," she said aloud, careening her bike around the curve of a parkside trail, "then Caleb plays Romeo and we put someone else in for Caleb's part and we create a situation in which any actor could be asked to play any role at any time." She shifted into a higher gear. "Like the swapped potion bottles and the props table. The actors don't know what to expect."

She shifted again. "No, the *entire company* doesn't know what to expect." Larkin couldn't forget about her production team—all of whom could, in theory, be suspects. "It puts everybody off their game. It prevents them from being their Best Selves."

Larkin wasn't sure that everybody in the company wanted to be their Best Selves, not in the way that she wanted to be—but she knew what happened when people were asked to work at less than their best. "It would have distracted us. Maybe it did distract us."

So Larkin begged the question, exactly the way her mother had taught her. "What did it distract us *from*?"

That was the kind of question that was difficult to answer—because if Larkin knew what she'd been distracted from seeing, she wouldn't have been distracted from seeing it. "I need to ask Anni," she said, gasping slightly, her legs begging for glucose and her lungs begging for air. "She'll see what I missed because she wasn't there to miss it."

Larkin slowed to a stop, swiping the sweat from her forehead. She was four miles from home, give or take. She could keep pedaling forward, circling the town until she ended up where she began, or she could retrace her path—and her thoughts.

Her first thought was that there was something she was forgetting.

Her second thought—the first one that came to mind, when she turned her bike around—was that she could ask Anni about it later.

Her third thought, as she heard the Howell College bell tower chime, was that *later* was going to be *sooner than she realized*.

———

"Sorry I'm late," Larkin said. Her hair was damp, since she'd only had time to rub herself down with a towel after getting out of the shower. Her T-shirt was also damp, since it had absorbed all of the water that had not made it onto the towel. She had no idea whether she was being her Best Self or not. She was, for the time, *being*.

"You're not that late," Anni said. "Not even ten whole minutes." She had already purchased her mug of ginger tea and her apple. Elliott had Earl Grey and the Ploughman's Platter; a chunk of housemade bread, two hard-boiled eggs, an array of local cheeses, and a slice of Iowa ham. He passed one of the eggs to Anni, who placed it carefully on a napkin.

"I could get you an extra plate," Larkin said.

"If you go anywhere near the kitchen where you used to work, they're going to ask you to pick up a shift," Anni said.

"Fair enough," Larkin said. "But you'd better hope that whoever restocked those napkins washed their hands first."

Anni stiffened—but only for an instant. Then she relaxed. "I'm getting better," Anni said. Larkin could see the effort she was making to release her tension. "Kitchens are going to be a problem for Elliott and me, so I need to develop a set of heuristics that allow me to quickly assess any sanitation concerns." She carefully examined her egg. "I am not a fan of heuristics. They are, by definition, short-cuts, which means they're suboptimal, but the Pareto Principle prevails."

"I think I understood 20 percent of that," Larkin said.

"Well played," Elliott said, raising his mug of tea.

"You know what I mean," Anni said, as Ed returned to the table with his vegetable panini and Larkin's banana-and-peanut-butter panini. His tray also contained one mug of lavender tea and the largest cup of coffee The Coffee Shop sold.

"The odds of my getting food poisoning from eating this egg are extremely small," Anni continued, taking a bite of the egg to prove her point, "but worrying about the odds causes small but measurable physical damage." She took another bite, careful not to let the yolk crumble out of its albumen. "Also psychological damage, which is to say *physical tension that increases the probability of future physical tension*, and interpersonal damage, which is to say *physical tension that increases Elliott's physical tension.*"

"What did I miss?" Ed whispered.

"Anni's trying to decide whether to eat an egg," Larkin whispered back.

"This damage accrues over time, and is likely to cause more cumulative negative effects than anything that might result from a single unpleasant gastrological event," Anni said, before popping the rest of the egg into her mouth. "Unless, of course—"

"That's the event that does you in," Elliott said, finishing Anni's sentence as she swallowed her mouthful. "Which brings us to the problem that Larkin is currently trying to solve."

"Who done him in?" Ed asked, in his best Audrey Hepburn.

"Well played," Elliott said again.

"Except that's not the problem I'm trying to solve," Larkin said, wiping her peanut-butter-sticky fingers on her napkin and then reaching across the table for the napkin that had held Anni's egg. "I think the more important problem is, you know, *what does the murderer want.*"

"You mean," Elliott said, looking at Larkin as if he were asking her a leading question, "why did they do it?"

"No," Larkin said. She looked at Anni. "You get the distinction between *why someone does something* and *what they hope to get from doing it*, right?"

"Absolutely," Anni said. "Action and result."

"That's where we have to start," Larkin said. "With the result."

"What actually happened," Elliott said, "and whether that was what the murderer wanted to happen."

"And if it was—" Larkin began.

"Then we ask ourselves who benefits," Ed said.

"And if it wasn't—" Larkin continued.

"Then we ask ourselves what the murderer is going to do next," Anni said, "to achieve the result they didn't get the first time."

"Or maybe the second time," Larkin concluded. "We've got two dead bodies now, and Farah Emerson is worried that she's going to be the third."

"Which one's Farah?" Elliott asked.

"Our Juliet," Larkin said. "She's the one who picked up the real dagger off the props table, and almost stabbed herself with it before she realized."

"Right," Elliott said. "We were there." Larkin had almost forgotten that. They'd all been there, at that first dress rehearsal—Josephine and Claire, Anni and Elliott, Sahil and Rupa and Jay Malhotra. They'd all sat within sight of each other. They'd all seen what had happened.

"And which one was the second body?" Anni asked.

"Amelia Jorgensen," Larkin said. "Our former Juliet."

"Who was fired from the company," Ed said, "along with our former artistic director Manny Morris, after the two of them were caught having an affair."

Manny had been at the first dress rehearsal too. So had Amelia. So had Clarissa Bankshaw Morris. They had sat behind Larkin, in the back of the amphitheater. Rebecca had sat with them, until the second intermission. Then, she'd moved up to sit with Larkin and Peg.

"Was she poisoned too?" Anni asked.

"She was stabbed," Larkin said, "with Juliet's dagger. The real one."

"She also left a suicide note," Ed said.

"A confession note," Larkin corrected. "She wrote *I did it*."

"Did what?" Anni asked.

"I think it just said *it*," Larkin said. She hadn't been able to take a picture of Amelia's note. She hadn't been able to write it down. She was relying entirely on a memory that had been created in a moment of psychological tension—and the probability that she'd misremembered was creating so much physical tension, in the current moment, that her hands were shaking.

"Too much coffee, Larkin Day?"

It was Jay. Of course it was Jay. He'd found them, somehow—not that it would have been hard, Ed's car was parked out front and The Coffee Shop had plate glass windows, but still.

"What are you doing here?" Larkin asked.

Jay pulled up a chair as if he belonged at their table. Anni scootched her own chair slightly closer to Elliott and began tapping her fingers against his wrist.

"Is that Morse code?" Jay asked. "That's adorable. I don't know anything beyond S-O-S, so feel free to continue your private conversation. I assume it's about me." He held out his hand to Elliott. "Dr. Jaipal Malhotra." Jay and Elliott shook hands like sportsmen. "Most people call me Jay. People used to call you Scarbo, if I recall?"

Elliott hated being reminded of his former career as a professional magician—but he recognized Jay's move for what it was and responded in kind. "Yes," Elliott said. "You must have watched my television show." He emphasized *watched* just enough to let them all know that he had both considered and rejected *seen*. "Some people just saw the last episode."

It was an extremely clever way to ask the question. Jay would either have to admit that he had made time for Elliott's show while it was on network television—which would give Elliott the advantage, in terms of status—or that he had deliberately chosen to watch the one episode where Scarbo faltered. It had been a career-ending disaster, and plenty of people had reveled in the unraveling. If Jay had been a vicarious participant, laughing at reaction videos and auto-tuned remixes, Elliott could claim a partial victory—or, at least, a slight upper hand.

"What a disaster," Jay said, refusing to answer. "You set the stage afire."

"*Et soudain il s'éteignait*," Elliott said, just as he had said it on television. "Scarbo was extinguished, and these days most people just call me Elliott."

Another strategic move—to continue discussing Scarbo at this point would be rude—and Jay responded by changing tactics. He tilted his chair onto its two back legs, supporting his feet against the cafe table. Taking up more than his share of the space. Forcing Anni to scootch even closer to Elliott.

Jay smiled. "You're with her, aren't you."

Larkin was both astonished and appalled at the way Jay had immediately identified both Elliott and Anni's insecurities. Elliott would always be the magician who burned down both his scrim and his career. Anni would always be the woman who had let Elliott go off to Hollywood by himself, ten years ago. She'd assessed her value as a potential asset, and now she watched Jay make the same assessment. Tiny, awkward, bespectacled, with a growing-out pixie cut clasped between a network of tiny barrettes shaped like houses. Jay might have been able to tell that Anni was brilliant—most people figured that out, sooner or later—but he had chosen to tell everyone that she was unattractive.

"We made an offer on a house this morning," Elliott said.

"That explains the—" Jay gestured towards Anni's barrettes. "Are those emoji?"

"And with interest rates being what they are," Anni said, ignoring the distraction and clutching Elliott's hand, "we decided to pay cash."

Jay, in his precarious chair, almost fell over. The failed magician and his unattractive girlfriend had money. Maybe not quite as much money as the Malhotras, but enough for them to buy a house without taking out a mortgage.

"Congratulations!" Ed said. He raised his mug of lavender tea, timing it to the rise of his eyebrows, turning his head towards Larkin to save face. They had known that Anni and Elliot were doing well financially—Larkin distinctly recalled Anni telling her CPA that she was earning six figures as a freelancer, and she less-distinctly recalled that Elliott did something with computers—but neither of them had expected Anni and Elliott to drop a quarter of a million dollars on a house, just like that.

Elliott's thumb twitched, back and forth, within Anni's grip. Morse code, again.

"I'll tell you what he said, since you don't know," Anni said. "He said *checkmate*."

"And now I'll tell you something you don't know," Jay said. "Amelia Jorgensen didn't stab herself."

"We already knew that," Larkin said.

"It was our primary hypothesis," Anni clarified. "So she was poisoned, then?"

"Wait," Jay said, "how did you—"

"Because we've done this before," Anni said, "and in one of our previous murder investigations, we learned that people tend to stick to whatever method they believe will work." She was referring to the first mystery she and Larkin had solved together. It had involved benzodiazepines. "People also do this in non-murder situations," Anni clarified. "We're behavior replicators, all the way down. In fact, most of us are behavior replicators on two different axes. We do what we've done previously, and we do what the people around us are doing." She sipped her tea. "Which means you've come here to help us solve the murders?"

"No," Elliott said. "Dr. Malhotra came here to throw Larkin off her game. Then he realized he would have to play me, instead—which is fascinating, Jay, how you assumed I was the highest-ranking person at this table— and he lost, and now he's going to tell us how he got all of this information before Larkin did."

"I'm a lead surgical resident," Jay said, angling his chair one last time for status, repeating the behavior that had just failed him. "I was suspicious of the position of the dagger as soon as I saw it, but I didn't want to say anything until I could confirm."

"But you're saying the stabbing wouldn't have killed her?" Ed asked. Larkin wondered why Jay hadn't assumed Ed was the highest-ranking person at the table. Ed was visibly impressive—the assistant professor, the choral director, the community leader, the gorgeous Black man with the soaring tenor voice—in a way that Elliott, who only ever looked like a stereotypical white nerd, was not.

"Whoever did it missed the heart and lungs completely," Jay said, returning all four feet of his chair to the floor. People found Ed impressive, but they also found him personable—which might have something to do with why Jay was treating Ed like a person.

"So it was cyanide, then," Larkin said.

"Yes, Inspector Day," Jay said. *Why wasn't he able to treat her like a person?*

"And now you're going to help us solve the murders," Anni said, again. "Even though you weren't, before."

"I—" Jay began.

"Yes, you are," Larkin said, "because you didn't come here to throw me off my game. Sorry, Elliott, but you don't know Jay like I do. He came here because I figured out his deal the day I met him, and he still hasn't figured out what my deal is." She smiled at Ed and Elliott and Anni, each of whom held their own—or their end, as Ed would put it— in her deal. She wondered if Jay had friends like hers. She wondered if that was what Jay wanted. She hoped Jay didn't just want *her*. "You know I'm right."

"Wrong," Jay said. He stood up, as if he had been planning his exit ever since he entered. "I came to tell you that Caleb Alderton, your understudy for Romeo, has resigned from the production. He was in my father's office this morning. Now he's on a bus back to Madison, or Indianapolis, or wherever these kids come from."

"Caleb's from Springfield," Ed said. "We could drive there. Beat the bus. Talk to him." Larkin could see the road trip beginning to take shape behind his eyes. He'd done so well, keeping Farah from leaving. He could do it again.

"Don't bother," Jay said. "The Board already voted. Opening Night is canceled."

CHAPTER 15

"Call Mitchell Davis," Larkin said, as soon as they were in the car. Ed was driving, Anni and Elliott were in the back seat. They were going to the Summer Shakespeare offices, in Cedar Rapids. Jay, in his tiny, shiny sportscar, was following them.

"I'm not sure I have Mitchell's number," Ed said. He was driving at exactly three miles above the speed limit, despite Jay's car's proximity to his car's bumper. Larkin watched other cars pass them, and knew that this whole deal—*her whole deal*—had to be driving Jay to distraction.

Not just the part where she and her boyfriend and her two best friends had piled into a car together, leaving Anni and Elliott's bikes locked to the rack in front of The Coffee Shop, but also the part where Larkin had told Jay that Opening Night would not be canceled.

"Call Ben Blankenship," Larkin said. This time the car connected.

"Larkin!" Ben said. "Everyone's fine, nobody's dead, Portia and Farah spent the morning doing each other's hair, I assume you want to talk to my husband?"

"You assume correctly," Larkin said. "You're on speaker, in Ed's car. Anni and Elliott are with us."

"I'll put you on speaker, too," Ben said. "Are you coming our way?"

"No," Larkin said. "We're going to CR. Mitchell, are you there?"

"Yes," Mitchell said. "I'm in the kitchen, Farah's with me—and before you ask, I voted not to cancel Opening Night."

"Good," Larkin said. "Because it's not going to be canceled. Not while I'm still Artistic Director." She squeezed Ed's hand. "Not while I've got such a good team."

"Who's going to play Romeo?" Farah asked.

"I'll figure that out," Larkin said, "before we open."

———

The four of them took the stairs to Sahil's office. They had seen Jay, in the lobby, waiting for them—but he was looking at his phone when they actually arrived, and so Larkin looked at Anni and Anni looked at the stairwell and up they went, leaving Jay by the elevators. It was just enough subterfuge to be amusing. Like their first mystery, before they knew what they were getting themselves into. Two millennial-aged women, playing detectives, with their tall, dark, and/or handsome boyfriends following behind. Never mind that two people had been killed. Never mind that Larkin still didn't know who'd killed them.

She did know what she needed to say, as soon as she opened the door to Sahil's office. Larkin had figured it out as she climbed the fourth flight.

"You let Caleb leave."

It was not a question. It was an accusation—and one that Sahil Malhotra was not expecting.

"He was angry," Sahil said. He glanced from Larkin to Ed, then to Anni and Elliott, whom he recognized but did not know. "He said he would not go onstage if he did not know who he would be playing against."

"And you let him leave."

"What else could I have done?"

"You could have brought me in," Larkin said. "I could have explained that this happens in professional theater all the time. Everyone knows more than one part. There are understudies and standbys and swings. Some people are hired specifically to learn all the parts, and to fill in for anyone at a moment's notice."

Sahil, for all his Shakespeare Festival experience, appeared not to have known this. He rearranged a few ink pens that had been standing in a handmade clay mug. Larkin wondered if Jay had made the mug when he was younger. She wondered where Jay was.

"We couldn't reach you," Sahil finally said. "We tried your phone."

"Which is still in the cabin where Amelia Jorgensen—" Larkin was about to say *where Amelia Jorgensen was found,* before she remembered that not everyone was aware of the distinction—and even if Sahil knew that Amelia had been poisoned before she was stabbed, he didn't know that Larkin knew it. "Where Amelia Jorgensen died."

"Of course," Sahil said, as if that explained everything. "So you see we had no choice."

"Your son chose to find me," Larkin said. "He seemed to have very little trouble."

That was when Jay—who had been standing in the doorway, unnoticed—spoke. "It didn't take much detective work," he said. "I called Larkin's mother, and she said that Larkin and her friends were at The Coffee Shop."

Larkin thought about telling her mother not to give her location to anyone who asked, especially when she was in the middle of an active murder investigation—but she knew that it wouldn't have mattered, not in this case. Jay would have been able to manipulate her mother the same way he manipulated his father.

The same way he could be manipulating her, right now.

Did Jay want the show to go on?

If so, why?

"So you could have brought me into the meeting," Larkin said, continuing her interrogation, "but you chose not to."

Sahil pulled an ink pen out of the mug and placed it on the side of his desk. "It was an unprecedented situation."

"No, it wasn't," Larkin said. She was so tired of that word. "We precedented it last night, when Portia played Juliet." She glanced at Ed, then at Jay. They were both ready for her next move—and they both knew what it was.

Larkin looked directly at Sahil. "I could find us another Romeo."

Sahil twisted the pen from parallel to perpendicular. Then he picked it up again. "Who?"

"Ed can play Romeo," Larkin said.

Ed smiled. He'd been expecting this. Anni and Elliott had been expecting this, too. "Put me in, coach," he said.

"Do you know the part?" Sahil asked.

"I could make it through," Ed said. "We could do what we did with Portia and give me a way to read the lines."

"We're not doing that again," Sahil said. "We don't need another lead actor hiding behind paper fans." He looked at Larkin. "Who do you know who knows the part?"

Larkin's next glance was towards Elliott—but the former stage magician shook his head.

She looked at Jay, but all he did was raise an insouciant eyebrow.

She considered, for just an instant, taking on the role herself. Nobody would believe she was a boy, of course, not even with a quadruple-strength sports bra. On the other hand, the idea had marketing potential, especially since they might have trouble selling tickets to a play that had lost not only its first but also its second Romeo. *Come see the former Artistic Director take on the lead role—*

"Manny Morris," Larkin said. "He'll do it."

He *could* and he *would*—and everybody knew it.

"He can't play Romeo," Sahil said. "He's too old."

"So was Olivier," Larkin said, "when he played Hamlet."

"So was Robeson," Ed said, "when he played Othello."

"So was Branagh," Elliott said, "when he played Benedick."

"So was Mel Gibson," Jay said. "He was almost the same age as the woman who played his mother."

"We're all older than people used to be," Anni said, "when they did things."

"And if your camp requires seventeen-year-olds to be supervised at all times," Larkin concluded, "you get fifty-year-old Romeos. That's how it works."

Larkin watched Sahil consider this.

"I suppose Manny would enjoy being close to his daughter," he finally said.

"Manny will enjoy playing the lead role and that's all that matters," Larkin said. "He'll also love that you called him, *personally*, and asked him for help. By the time we open tonight, everyone in the theater community will know exactly what happened. You'll sell every ticket you haven't yet sold, just so people can watch the disgraced artistic director save the day."

"We already sent the email," Sahil said, "canceling tonight's performance."

"Perfect," Larkin said. "That means you get to send a new one. With the announcement." She smiled. "Make sure you use the words *the show must go on*."

Then she turned to her friends. "Ed," Larkin said, "you're coming with me. We'll pick up Portia and Farah, meet Manny at the campsite, and start to rehearse." She glanced back at Sahil. "You can get Manny on camp by three, right?"

There were two clocks in Sahil's office—a corporate one mounted above the door and a marble one planted on his desk—but he automatically reached for his phone. It was 1:35. "I suppose," he said. "If he isn't busy."

"Trust me," Larkin said. "He'll drop everything for this." She shifted her gaze to Anni. "Can you and Elliott ride with Jay? He'll take you back to The Coffee Shop, and then you can take Elliott's car to camp." She gave Jay an echo of his insouciant grin. He couldn't deny her request, not in front of his father, not if he wanted to be like his mother.

"Yes," Anni said. "Jay's car is extremely safe. It has to be, since statistically the people who drive those kinds of cars are less likely to follow the rules of the road."

Larkin watched Sahil stiffen. "But you're a safe driver, Jaipal."

"The safest," Jay said. He put his hand on his father's shoulder until it relaxed. "Call Manny. Send your email. I'll take these two back to that coffee shop—you should see it, Dad, it's adorable—and then I'll join you all at camp." He winked at Larkin. "I assume that's where you want me?"

"Yes," Larkin said. "In one hour. With your fiancée, her internet access, and two burner smartphones."

————

They met, outside the mess hall, at 2:30. Ed, Portia, Farah, Larkin, Jay, Beatrix, Elliott, and Anni. Jay carried a plastic shopping bag. Elliott wore a backpack with a padded slot for his laptop, and Anni had her canvas utility bag. She'd also swapped her barrettes, and now her hair was held back by two tiny theater masks. Comedy on the right side, tragedy on the left. "We don't know which way the night is going to go, you see," she explained.

Larkin had a pretty good idea of how she wanted the night to go—and she was ready to do everything it took to make it happen.

"We'll start with the phones," she said, holding out her hand to Jay. He gave her the shopping bag, and she took out one of the plastic clamshells and handed it to Ed.

"Of course," Jay said. "Because Ed's phone is also locked up in the cabin where Amelia—"

"Right," Larkin said, before Jay could finish his sentence in a way any of them might regret. She took out the second clamshell and attempted to tear it apart with her hands. Anni reached into her utility bag and handed her a pair of tiny scissors.

"Thanks," Larkin said, freeing her phone and Ed's, jamming the plastic into the shopping bag and passing it back to Jay. "Do we all have phones?"

Ed held his up, the blue light glowing off the freshly powered display. Portia followed. So did Farah, Elliott, Anni, and Beatrix. Jay was the last person to take his phone out of his pocket, using the moment to demand an extra bit of Larkin's attention.

What did Jay want?

Why wasn't he able to treat her like a person?

"Great," Larkin said. "Now—"

She turned to Beatrix.

"Show us how to connect to the solar-powered Wi-Fi router."

The process was not very difficult. Beatrix had set up a hidden network—"to keep all of your phones, and all of you, from asking to connect with it," she explained—and once she allowed them onto her network, it was simply a matter of passing out the password.

"The Wi-Fi password is TestTest123?" Elliott asked. "That's not very secure."

"It doesn't matter if it's secure if nobody knows it exists," Beatrix replied. She had picked up a bit of spark, Larkin noticed, to match her sparkling engagement ring.

"Well," Elliott said, tapping at his phone and then quickly looking around the circle of people, "now there are eight of us who know it exists. We also know how to access it."

"I have to give you access," Beatrix said. "From my phone."

"Yes, I know," Elliott said. "That's the point."

Anni was the only one who understood what he meant, probably because Elliott transmitted it to her through a series of dots and dashes. Not on her wrist, not with Jay watching. On the side of her foot, perhaps, while Portia strapped the tracking device around Farah's ankle. It had originally been designed for a child's wrist —bright pink, with a watch face shaped like a smiling cat—but that would be too obvious, both on and off stage.

"As long as you keep your socks scrunched like that," Larkin said, "it won't show."

Farah understood. "And when we perform, I'll be able to hide it under Juliet's skirts and hose."

"Which means you'll need to be careful in the dressing room," Portia said, "and in the shower."

"It's waterproof," Elliott said. "We made sure of that when we bought it."

"Water resistant," Anni corrected. After Jay had dropped them off at The Coffee Shop, they had ridden their bikes back to Anni's apartment and then taken Elliott's car to one of the big-box stores outside Cedar Rapids. "Up to thirty meters."

"If I end up underneath thirty meters of water," Farah said, "we're going to have other problems."

"That's not what *water-resistant-up-to-thirty-meters* means," Anni said, "but it doesn't matter. We'll know if you leave the campsite. We'll know if your heart stops beating. We'll also know if the watch stops working."

"What happens if she takes the watch off?" Beatrix asked. "Does it code as *heart stops beating*?"

"Yes," Elliott said. "And we all get notified."

"Who's *we*?" Farah asked. "Everyone here?"

"No," Elliott said. "We need redundancy, of course, but not so much redundancy that it compromises our security. Only four of us have parent access—myself, Anni, Larkin, and Ed."

"Is that—" Farah asked.

"Exactly what it sounds like," Elliott confirmed.

"Why can't we all be Farah's mommies and daddies?" Jay asked.

"The app only had four parent slots," Elliott said. "The designers must have had limited experience with what constitutes a family."

Then Elliott sent Anni another Morse Code message. Larkin was sure of it. He had his arm around her waist, which neither of them had ever done before, at least not while anyone was watching. Ed put his arm around Larkin's waist—*kinesthetic response*, Larkin thought, automatically—and whispered in her ear.

"Everything's going to be all right," he said. "Everything's going according to plan."

"That's not the same thing," Larkin whispered back.

They dispersed, after that—Beatrix to inform the company about the change of plans, Portia to warm the cast up for an afternoon of rehearsal, Elliott and Anni to watch Farah's movements from the apartment in Pratincola, Larkin and Ed to the front gate to welcome Manny Morris when he arrived. Jay, suddenly superfluous, followed them.

"Do you know what Anni told me?" he asked.

"What?" Larkin said. Jay's voice had changed, slightly, when he said *Anni*. He had moved her, in his mind, into the category of *people he needed to treat like people*.

"She told me what she had tapped onto her magician boyfriend's wrist," Jay said, "when I showed up at The Coffee Shop earlier today."

"You mean Elliott," Ed said.

"Yes, Elliott, Scarbo, whatever," Jay said. He crossed his arms over his chest, uncomfortably, in the summer heat. Then he uncrossed them. "Anni said that she and I were both one-axis people in a two-axis world." Jay imitated Anni's voice, the way he had imitated his mother's. "You and I are only behavior replicators on one axis, which is why we have a hard time interacting with people."

"Which means, like—" Larkin was watching the gravel road for Manny's car.

"She means that the two of us only care about the way

our behaviors interface with our own goals," Jay said. "We don't do things to go along with the group." He did Anni's voice again, almost perfectly. "But Larkin and Ed and Elliott don't ever make me feel like I have to do what they're doing, especially when what they're doing is inefficient, which is why we're friends."

Ed laughed. "That sounds like Anni."

"Is that good or bad?" Larkin asked. She was still only half paying attention.

"The fact that Jay can mimic like that?" Ed said. "Very good. Especially if you're thinking about doing *Comedy of Errors* next year. You could cast him as one of the twins."

"It's *Winter's Tale* next year," Larkin said. "It's already been decided."

"And I'm no actor," Jay said. "Acting is a two-axis career."

That was when they saw the car—and saw, almost immediately afterwards, that it wasn't Manny's. It was Anni and Elliott, Anni rolling down the passenger-side window, half of her hair blowing into her face.

"One of my barrettes came out," she said. "Larkin, can you help me find it?"

"Sure," Larkin said.

"It's probably where we all were, with the phones," Anni said, hopping out of the car and walking off with Larkin as if there were nothing more important, in the entire world, than finding the comedy half of her theatrical hairclips. Ed knew there was something going on. Jay might have, except Elliott—Larkin saw, as she glanced over her shoulder—was distracting him.

"Elliott's letting him have the advantage, for like two seconds," Anni said. "Also, my barrette is in my pocket."

"Great," Larkin said. They were halfway to the mess hall, at a curve in the path that put them temporarily out of view—but not necessarily out of earshot, which is why Anni whispered.

"We're not the only people who have access to Beatrix's Wi-Fi."

"How do you know?"

"Because Elliott wrote a script, before we drove over here, to identify and locate the users on any network his phone was currently connected to."

"Can you do that?"

"No," Anni said, "but Elliott can."

Larkin let that pass without comment. "So who else has access?"

"We don't know," Anni said. "It's a smart burner, like yours. But whoever it is—"

"Whoever has that phone—"

"Is currently on the campground."

CHAPTER 16

Larkin knew, as she walked with Anni back to the front gate, that she had to focus.

"Elliott and I will track User Nine," Anni had said, "while we track Farah."

"From Pratincola?"

"Of course not," Anni said. "We were never going all the way back to Pratincola. We'll hide out at the pond where you and Ed have lunch. Just five minutes away."

A lot could happen in five minutes—and a lot, as Larkin saw, already had. Manny had arrived, and Ed had taken over the welcoming duties. Jay's attention was divided between Manny, who had status with the Festival, and Elliott, who had status with the group. As soon as he saw Larkin, Jay understood that her status had also increased. She had information that he did not, and as Larkin walked past Jay and extended her hand to Manny, she watched Jay realize that she was not going to tell him what she knew.

"We're so glad that you could help us out," Larkin said, clasping Manny's hand before giving it a firm shake. "I know you've played the part before, and I know you've seen our rehearsals, so I'm hoping we'll be able to put this together fairly quickly."

"Me too," Manny said. Then he looked directly into Larkin's eyes, the same way she looked at her actors before she asked them to do something difficult. "I know you've probably heard a few things about me, and maybe some of them are true." His face twisted into chagrin, then relaxed into a smile. "But I love the theater. I love this Festival. I love the process that goes into making art—and I think you'll find, over the next few hours, that I'm a professional through-and-through."

This turned out to be true. Manny Morris was more than amenable, integrating himself into the role without making unnecessary suggestions or requesting time-consuming alterations. He already knew the lines, which was helpful—but he also understood both the blocking and the timing in a way that Larkin hadn't anticipated. She sat next to Camryn, the two of them looking over the notes the assistant stage manager had taken during the early rehearsals, and nearly every time Camryn would start to say something like "cross downstage left" or "look at Juliet," Manny would have already done it.

"That's how I would have directed it," he explained, the first time Camryn stopped mid-sentence. The second time he said "that's the best way to do it." After that they let Shakespeare speak, without comment, until it was time for their ten-minute break. Then, as Larkin was expecting —and, perhaps, hoping—Manny Morris came directly towards her.

"You are doing extremely well," he said. "I'd make a

joke about *given the circumstances,* but you appear to be surpassing your circumstances."

"As are you," Larkin said. "I mean, given your circumstances. I mean, I'm sorry for your loss." She was aware, out of the corner of her eye, that Jay was watching her. Looking for an opening. Waiting for his chance to distract her from the work she needed to do.

"Amelia?" Manny said. "You know, I didn't know she had passed until Sahil called me."

"Wow," Larkin said. "I mean, I am sorry." This time she actually was.

"Mr. and Mrs. Jorgensen must not have been aware of the extent of your relationship with their daughter," Jay said, stepping between the two Artistic Directors, presenting the sentence as if it could have been sincere.

"Nobody was," Manny said. Then he turned to leave, mumbling some pablum about bathrooms.

"I want to talk to you later," Larkin called after him, hoping it sounded like an apology.

"I want to talk to you now," Jay said. It sounded like a warning.

"What," Larkin hissed, "is your deal?"

"We've already established," Jay hissed back, mimicking Larkin's tone and timbre, "that you know exactly what my deal is. I am the one who does not understand your deal, which now includes the fact that you have information relevant to our mystery that you have not shared." He ran a hand through his curls. "Even though I drove all the way out to that charming little coffee shop to tell you what I knew about Amelia's death."

"It wasn't that far of a drive," Larkin said. After spending five years in Los Angeles, where a seven-mile journey could take two hours, the fifteen minutes it took to drive from Cedar Rapids to Pratincola was laughably negligible. Larkin and Anni had done it on their bikes, once, using the network of trails and protected bike lanes that linked the Creative Corridor. That had taken—

"You're not paying attention," Jay said.

"You're right," Larkin said. "What did you want me to pay attention to?"

She watched the word appear in front of Jay's eyes.

Me.

Then she watched him decide not to say it.

"Break is over," Camryn said. "Places for act 3, scene 1."

Jay looked at Larkin. They both knew that he had been presented with an opportunity to be his Best Self—even if he didn't think of it in those terms—and they both knew that he had rejected the gift.

"Be careful, Larkin Day," Jay said. "I only ever wanted to be your friend."

That was a lie.

"Now I may have to become your enemy."

That—Larkin realized—was true.

———

After rehearsal, Larkin invited Manny to dinner. None of those words meant anything close to what they might have meant, off the Festival campsite, on a non-Opening Night. There was nowhere they could go but the mess hall. There was nothing either of them cared to eat, although they each ended up grabbing a plastic-wrapped protein bar—Manny picked blueberry, Larkin picked peanut-butter-chocolate—and a fresh bottle of water. There was no real way for them to separate themselves from the crowd, no private rooms, no tables for two, not until Manny nodded and Larkin followed and the two of them left the mess hall and the path and began picking their way through a cluster of trees.

"Make sure to check yourself for ticks," Manny said. He sounded, for a minute, like a father—and Larkin tried to remember the last time she'd spoken to his daughter. Rebecca had been at the rehearsal, sandwiched between Isabella, who was gazing at Manny like she was ready to take Amelia's place, and Peg, who had taken over the job of ensuring Rebecca was always within someone's sightlines. Larkin could have asked, then, how Rebecca was doing—her father's girlfriend found dead on the floor of their cabin, her father taking over the lead role—but she hadn't even thought of it. She'd been distracted by Manny, and Jay, and the mystery, and Shakespeare.

"How's Rebecca doing?" Asking Manny wasn't the same thing as asking Rebecca, but it was a start.

"She's doing fine," Manny said. Now he really sounded like a father—because he didn't know, and he had also forgotten to ask, and since Rebecca hadn't done anything to attract his attention, he was going to assume everything was okay. Larkin thought of her own father, the few afternoons they'd spent together when Larkin was a toddler, her dad bringing her back to her mom's apartment, saying everything had gone well. It never had—but Larkin had been good at playing pretend, even then. Everyone who ended up in theater started out playing pretend. Some of them never stopped.

"Here we are," Manny said.

Here was a tree with a battered wooden bench leaning against the trunk. Weather-worn, hidden from view, so far off the path that there weren't even footprints to follow. A secret that was only ever passed from one person to another.

"How did you find this?" Larkin asked.

"I built it," Manny said. "The first summer I played Romeo."

"Wow," Larkin said. "How old were you?"

"Sixteen," Manny said. He sat down. Larkin sat next to him. The bench, as dilapidated as it looked from a distance, did not wobble.

"I lost my virginity on this bench," Manny said.

Larkin almost stood up—but she understood that this wasn't the right moment to make a joke.

"Not to our Juliet, of course," Manny said. "To our director."

Larkin almost said something—*I'm sorry*—but she understood that this wasn't even the right moment to react. This moment, this scene that Manny had directed them into, was about the sharing of this story.

"I'm sure you understand that things were different, back then," Manny said. "Nobody would have been let go from their job for something as quotidian as adultery." He unscrewed the cap of his water bottle. "Especially not an Artistic Director."

Larkin almost wanted to apologize, again—but she understood that this was not what Manny wanted from her.

"And Amelia was twenty-one," Manny said. "Much older than I was, when it first happened to me." He took a sip of water. "I was sixteen. The next year it was a different director, and I was seventeen. The year after that it was a professor, and I got to play Puck in *Midsummer*. After that everyone just thought I was good."

He looked at Larkin. "And I was." He looked at the bench he had built, between his legs. "I mean, I was determined to be good. To prove that I was more than a pretty piece of flesh, to quote our Bard." He looked at Larkin again. "They wouldn't have introduced me to so many people if I weren't."

He stood up. Took a few steps away from the tree, turned around. Exactly how both of them would have blocked it. "It's not what people think it is," Manny said, "or at least it wasn't, back then. It was what everyone understood that everyone was doing. They were testing our mettle. Seeing how we responded. In many ways it was the platonic expression of the trust fall." He looked away. "And of course everybody used condoms."

He looked back at Larkin, expecting her to say *of course*, expecting them both to understand that it wasn't true. Instead, she said "But it's different now."

"It is," Manny said. "I was always told that it would be *quid pro quo*. I put in my quid, became a pro, and then the quo changed."

Larkin almost felt sorry for Manny. Then she thought of Amelia, acting out a part that had already been cut from the script. "Did you teach her what they taught you?" Manny's eyes jerked towards Larkin, then towards his feet, then—as if God, Shakespeare, and the dead were watching—towards the sky.

"No," Manny said. "You know that."

"Why not?"

"Because she wasn't good enough," Manny said. "The good ones—anyone with real talent—they don't play that game anymore."

Larkin no longer felt sorry for Manny. "Who says you get to decide who's good?"

"Because I understand the standard," Manny said. "And if she'd had what it takes to achieve that standard, if she'd wanted to do the work, on herself, you know—" He looked at the ground again. A secret, shared and buried.

"She wouldn't have offed herself the first time she didn't get what she wanted."

If Larkin had felt anything for Manny—kindness, respect, anything at all—she might have told him that Amelia's death hadn't been a suicide. Instead, she let him think that Amelia had expected something of him that he had not been willing to give. She let him think that Amelia had killed Tyler, attempted to kill Farah, and then killed herself. She let him think that all of this had happened because he had decided that Amelia wasn't good enough. Larkin watched him pace and turn, consider and reconsider.

Then he sat down on the bench again.

"You're as good as I would have been," Manny said. "Maybe better."

"You've decided that?" Two hours ago she'd wanted Manny's approval. Now she didn't care.

"The work decided it," Manny said. "You keep making the best choices."

"How do you know they're the best?" Larkin asked. "Because they're the choices you would have made?"

"No," Manny said. "Because every choice you make supports the production you're creating."

Larkin understood, immediately, what he meant. It was one of the hardest things to do, as a director. To envision the kind of production you wanted to create. To present the production to a company in a way that allowed them to help you create it. To ensure that every choice, made by every actor and designer and choreographer and musical director, supported the presentation. To say no, when it was hard. To say yes, when it was harder.

"Like this choice," Larkin said. "To bring you back, so the show could go on."

"To listen to me," Manny said, "so the show could go on."

He understood—of course he understood—that Larkin did not like him.

He also understood that they were both working towards the same goal.

So they stood up, left the bench without looking back, and walked out of the woods together.

That was when Larkin's phone, zipped into the part of her backpack that pressed against her back, began vibrating. Larkin hadn't planned for this—what to do if your secret burner phone starts making noise when there's someone else around—so she began singing. The tenor solo at the end of Beethoven's Ninth Symphony, since it was the first thing that came to mind.

"That's Ode to Joy, isn't it," Manny said. "Wasn't there a big deal about that, with the combined orchestra and chorus, last fall?"

"I was in it," Larkin said. "Chorus." Her phone vibrated one more time, then stopped. "Did you go?"

"No," Manny said. "We had tickets, but then my marriage fell apart."

He said it like it was something that happened by accident.

"I suppose that would have been different, too," Larkin said. "In the old days. You could have had your wife and your child and your protégé all at once."

"I still have my child," Manny said, and then he walked away from Larkin—which was fine, because all she wanted to do was get him out of sight so she could look at her phone.

The texts were from Anni.

hello

this is anni

farah is fine, heartbeat and location stable
another phone just connected to the hidden wi-fi network
elliott did his hacker magic
he says that taking advantage of bad infosec isn't really hacking
anyway
this phone belongs to clarissa bankshaw morris

CHAPTER 17

Larkin didn't even have time to put her phone into her backpack before it buzzed again.

another user

elliott is investigating

She looked ahead—Manny, gone, between the trees. She looked behind her, trying to remember the quickest path from the bench to the campsite. She looked at her phone, which was once again vibrating.

three more

four

five

many

elliott is getting names

Larkin texted back.

Tell Elliott not to bother.

It's going to be everybody.

Then she started running.

CHAPTER 18

Larkin knew exactly what to expect, when she arrived back on the campsite—but it was, somehow, even worse than she was expecting.

Actors, sprawled about the amphitheater in various stages of unpreparedness. Crew, wiping frosting-stained fingers on black pants as they munched pre-packaged cake rolls from the mess hall. Every face illuminated. Every head tilted. Every pair of eyes on their own screen. Their own stream—flowing, as streams do, from a single source.

"You gave them the internet," Larkin said.

Jay held up his own phone. Took a photo. Uploaded it. "It was the least I could do," he said. "Since we have a functional Wi-Fi network and all." He showed the social media post to Larkin. "Do you like the caption?"

He had labeled the photo—sixty people, staring at their devices—*ninety minutes 'till curtain.*

Larkin's phone buzzed. Anni, again.

connection to Farah has started to lag
too many people using internet

elliott says this isn't a usual case, the network should be able to handle it

except everyone is downloading four weeks of email all at once

and everyone's phone is installing automatic updates

lots of packets going back and forth

and the Farah-tracking app can't maintain real-time telemetry

"See?" Jay said. "Even you."

He showed Larkin the photo he had just posted. A sweaty-looking woman, her forehead twisted, eyes focused only on her phone. *Our director, hard at work.*

Farah is fine, Larkin texted—because there she was, socks pulled over her ankle bracelet, laughing at the latest memes. Ed was next to Farah, using the smart burner Elliott had bought him, texting his own messages—so Larkin put her burner phone back into her pocket and got her boyfriend's attention the old-fashioned way.

"Ed!" Larkin called out, waving her arms over her head. His eyes immediately met hers; he began walking over.

"Is this my cue to go?" Jay asked.

"Directors don't give cues," Larkin said. "Only stage managers." She waved, again, at Ed. "Do you have the keys to the tech booth?" she shouted.

"Always," Ed called back, patting his pocket.

"Good," Larkin said. She turned back to Jay. "You know I'll lock the door behind us."

"I'll let you make your move," Jay said. "It's only fair."

Larkin didn't understand why Jay was suddenly playing fair. She still didn't understand what Jay wanted. A few hours ago, he had helped them un-cancel Opening Night. Now he was trying, deliberately, to ruin everything they had worked towards.

———

"I need you to turn on the sound system," Larkin said, once she and Ed had ascended the stairs to the tech booth, "and get ready to hand me the God Mic."

"I'll get the sound going," Ed said, "but only Velvet can use the God Mic."

"You're right," Larkin said. "Thanks." If she wanted a company of professionals, she had to act like one—and she had to surround herself with people who would accept nothing less. Behavior replicates on two axes, just like Anni had said. "Can you go find her?" She looked at Ed. "Sorry. I don't mean to give you orders."

"It's okay," Ed said. "I can tell you're a little distracted right now."

Larkin looked at her phone. No new messages. She looked out the tech booth window. Farah was still exactly where she was supposed to be. She looked at her phone again. *Eighty-six minutes 'till curtain.* "Sorry," she said again.

"This is why we have stage managers," Ed said, kissing her forehead and grabbing his keys. "I'll be right back."

It only took a moment for Ed to return with Velvet—which took them down to *eighty-three minutes.* "It's about time we got internet," Velvet said, grinning as she held up a picture of a grandbaby.

"It's the worst time to get internet," Larkin said, a little too quickly. Velvet, crushed, tapped the picture away. "Sorry," Larkin said. "I mean—"

She asked herself *what Velvet wanted.*

"We have a situation," Larkin said, "that needs your expertise."

Velvet, who had only ever stage-managed community theater productions, was well aware that none of the production team viewed her as someone with *expertise*. Experience, yes—but not enough to demand a professional-level paycheck. Jiro had joked, once, that Velvet's job could easily be performed by a robot. "Artificial intelligence can understand audio and scan video," he had said. "There's no reason an AI couldn't run a show."

But Jiro had, once again, ignored the value of the people around him. Larkin would not—and Velvet knew it. "What do you want me to do, boss?" she asked, putting her phone in her pocket and settling herself into her stage manager's chair.

"Get the company's attention," Larkin said, gesturing towards the God Mic without touching it. "Tell them that we will be doing a group warmup in five minutes. Tell them—"

Larkin paused. She had been about to make another wrong move. "What do you think we should do," she asked Velvet, "to make sure everyone stays off their phones until the show's over? What do they do at the community theater?"

"We have a box," Velvet said. "At thirty minutes until curtain, the assistant stage manager goes around and collects all of the phones. Makes sure they're all turned off. Then the box sits on this shelf, next to where the ASM sits during the show, until the show's over."

Larkin nodded. "Does that work? Can we do that now?"

"I guess we'd need a box," Velvet said. She looked around the tech booth. It was remarkably uncluttered, not counting the tangle of headsets and cables that always accompanied tech workers. No food wrappers, though—and no empty boxes. "You could get one from the props shed," Velvet suggested. "We could send Rebecca and Camryn."

"Perfect," Larkin said. She had been ready to suggest that they send Ed, but was even more ready to defer to Velvet's expertise. "Can we tell the cast that we're going to take the phones away an hour before curtain? Since it's Opening Night and all."

"I was just about to say the same thing," Velvet said. She gave Larkin a smile that was even bigger than the one she'd given her phone. "Anything else we need to tell 'em?"

Larkin looked at Ed, hoping he'd tell her if she were making a tactical error. "I think we should thank Beatrix Yang for setting up and testing the Wi-Fi network, and thank the Festival for giving us all access to the internet."

"Sure," Ed said. "That way, it doesn't seem like we're taking away everyone's new toy."

"Right," Larkin said, even though that wasn't why she wanted to make the announcement. She wanted Jay to know that he hadn't ruined Opening Night. That she would win whatever game they were playing, because she had a team of people who were ready to help her.

"Sounds good," Velvet said. She picked up the God Mic, placed it in front of her, and turned it on. "Group warmup in five minutes," she said. "Five minutes until group warmup."

The company response was ingrained—and instant. "Thank you, five."

"I love theater people," Ed said.

"Now that I've got your attention, we have just a few announcements," Velvet continued. "You'll have plenty of time to look at those phones later, so please make sure and thank Beatrix Yang for setting up the Wi-Fi network. We'd also like to thank the Summer Shakespeare Festival for giving everyone access to the internet. Can we get a company cheer?"

As Velvet led the company in three rounds of *hip, hip, hooray,* Larkin realized just how much expertise—and experience—her stage manager had to offer. Velvet had unified the entire amphitheater in nine words. "Now for the other good news," Velvet continued. "We're going to make sure all of your phones stay safe during the show."

Larkin looked at Ed. *Brilliant,* she mouthed. *What?* Ed mouthed back—so she gave him two thumbs up, instead. They'd have to learn Morse Code, like Elliott and Anni had.

"Rebecca and Camryn are going to get us a box from the props shed," Velvet explained, "and we're going to have you turn off your phones—not silent, *completely off*—one hour before curtain. Those phones are going to sit right next to Camryn, downstage right, until the show's over. Then you can go right back to texting and ticky-tocking and whatever the kids are doing these days."

Velvet looked at Larkin. It wasn't the right way to end the speech, and both of them knew it. "Tell them that we've worked so hard on this show, especially this afternoon with the extra rehearsal, and we're so excited to give tonight's audience the best performance possible," Larkin said. "Then do one more round of that cheer."

Velvet repeated the statement, nearly verbatim, and Larkin and Ed joined in on the final *hooray!* Then Larkin squatted down, so her eyes would be level with Velvet's, and said "Thank you."

"It's just my job," Velvet said. "Now go do yours. We have—"

She checked the clock on the wall.

"Seventy-two minutes until curtain."

CHAPTER 19

Larkin didn't expect to run into Clarissa Bankshaw Morris immediately after exiting the tech booth, but she should have known that Manny's soon-to-be-ex-wife would be looming.

"I'm sorry about the internet thing," Clarissa said, as if she hadn't just heard the speech Velvet gave. "That one's my fault, I think. I saw Sahil's son using his phone, and I asked him where he was getting his Wi-Fi." She laughed. It was the kind of tinkly, wealthy laugh that people gave when they wanted to evade responsibility. "I told him that it was a good thing the entire company didn't have access, because it would be way too distracting." She laughed again. "But then he called Beatrix over—I can't believe they're engaged, by the way—and asked her to open the network to everyone! He said something about how it would be unfair to have something, especially information, and not share it."

"Right," Larkin said. Jay must have known that Clarissa would pass this anecdote along to her. He might even have asked her to do it. "Well, the cat's out of the bag.

Or the tubes. Or whatever." She watched Clarissa try to un-mix her metaphors. "I mean, we're going to be fine. Most workplaces have Wi-Fi, after all, and people still get things done."

"Oh, of course," Clarissa said. "But you know how theater people are. They don't think of this as a *workplace.* They think of it as a *family.*"

"Families have internet too," Larkin said. She was about to walk away, but Clarissa reached out and touched her arm. Both of them flinched; Larkin from the unexpected contact, Clarissa from the mix of sweat and sunscreen.

"Can you tell my daughter to turn on her phone?" Clarissa asked. "I don't know where Rebecca is right now."

"She's at the props shed," Larkin said, "with Camryn."

"No," Clarissa said, holding her phone towards Larkin. "I mean, my phone doesn't know where she is. Not if her phone isn't turned on."

Larkin was uninterested in mediating this conflict. "Talk to your daughter yourself," she said, walking down the amphitheater steps and towards the stage.

"I can't," Clarissa called after her, "not if I don't know how to find her."

———

Rebecca and Camryn appeared, with their box, during the group warmup. Larkin had already done her part, thanking the cast for their extra hours of rehearsal and leading a few simple stretches. Now it was Portia's turn— and everything was turnout and Alexander technique, the core exercises that would focus both their minds and their muscles.

"We couldn't find a black one," Camryn said, "but we were thinking about wrapping it in one of those black garbage bags from the mess hall. So it won't read."

Larkin nodded. If her eighteen-year-old assistant stage manager wanted to cover a cardboard box in black plastic to ensure that nobody in the audience could see it, she'd let her. "Do you have time?"

"Sure," Camryn said. She turned to Rebecca. "Let's go."

"Camryn." It was the voice of God—or Velvet, anyway, echoing over the amphitheater. "I need you on headset."

"Aww, nerts," Camryn said. Was that what the teens were saying these days? Or had Camryn's lack of access to the posts and videos that populated and popularized youth culture prompted her to recall her own catch-phrases? "I gotta go plug myself into the wall."

Rebecca laughed. Larkin should have paired Rebecca and Camryn together, put them in the same cabin, let them spend the summer giggling over teenage girl stuff—even though she knew, instinctively, that Clarissa Bankshaw Morris wouldn't have liked the idea of her daughter spending time with the likes of Camryn Kunkel. The girl was a *townie*, after all. Community theater. Community college. She'd go exactly as far as she already was, and it didn't matter if people like Clarissa needed people like Camryn to populate the cities where they built their businesses. To support them, answering their phones and cleaning their floors and, if they were lucky enough to have a little extra cash, putting it towards one of their financial schemes. Clarissa didn't understand that a person like Camryn would give five dollars to a roboadvisor every week, for the next twenty years, because she spent the best summer of her life hanging out with the daughter of the woman whose brother had developed the algorithm. All Clarissa Bankshaw Morris saw was her own daughter, sunburned and greasy-haired, wearing a sweat-stained T-shirt. Tying her curls back with a red bandana, because the local lesbian lighting designer—another *townie* —had been kind to her.

"I'll go with Peg," Rebecca said, waving at the woman in the matching bandana. "Since I gotta plug myself into another person."

She skipped off—actually *skipped*, as Camryn laughed —and Larkin stopped worrying about how Rebecca Bankshaw Morris was doing.

———

Rebecca's parents, on the other hand, needed some attention. Clarissa and Manny had found each other— which is to say that Clarissa had found Manny—and the two of them were in the middle of a conversation that neither of them had been expecting.

"Maybe I don't want you to come back," Clarissa was saying.

"I thought you did," Manny was replying. "I thought that was your singular goal."

Larkin was listening—and she realized, as soon as she felt his hand on her shoulder, that Stanley was listening as well. He and Susan had come up behind her, to stop her from going towards Clarissa and Manny.

"Let them be," the costume designer said. "They're learning a new dance."

"Good or bad?" Larkin asked.

"All new dances are good," the dramaturg said. "That's how we process—and how we progress."

Susan, with her British accent, had emphasized the *pro* in both *process* and *progress*. It made Larkin wonder if these two words were linked, somehow, to the idea of being a professional. She wanted to ask—Susan would know, she was sure of it—but was distracted by Beatrix.

"It's time for our Props Audit," Beatrix said, glancing between Larkin and—as was clearly reflected in her glasses—a checklist on her phone. "I can't find Rebecca."

"She's in the mess hall," Larkin said, "getting a black garbage bag."

"Is someone with her?" Susan asked. She and Stanley must have learned a new dance when they decided not to have children—or, maybe, a different kind of dance to process the fact that they couldn't.

"Peg's with Rebecca," Larkin said. She turned back to Beatrix. "Can you do the Props Audit without her?"

"We need three people," Beatrix said. "It's supposed to be me, Camryn, and Rebecca."

Larkin looked around the amphitheater to see if Isabella, their props master, could be of any use—but Isabella appeared to be using her *sixty-three minutes until curtain* to flirt with Jay and wait for Jiro to notice, and Larkin didn't want to go anywhere near them. "I'll fill in," Larkin said. "Let's go audit some props."

The two of them found Camryn, who was exactly where she should be—"I'm going off headset," Camryn said, into her microphone, before detaching herself from the headphones and cord that connected her to the tech booth—and began auditing the props. Larkin watched them pick up every item, confirming that nothing had been damaged or altered, ensuring everything was in the right place.

"Stage right props table clear," Camryn said.

"Stage right props table clear," Beatrix repeated, checking off an item on her phone. Then they crossed stage left.

The stage left props table was nearly identical to the stage right props table. Both of them were metal folding tables that had been covered with butcher paper. Someone —Isabella or Rebecca, most likely—had placed every prop on the table and then drawn a loose, freehand grid around each of the items. Some squares were larger than others, to accommodate bigger props. Some of them weren't even squares at all. Once the props had been arranged and the boundary lines drawn, each segment of the grid was labeled. *Nurse's handkerchief. Friar Laurence's basket. Juliet's dagger.*

Camryn held up a bottle. "Juliet's sleeping potion," she said. This was not the original bottle, nor was it the bottle that had been too big for Juliet's girdle. It was a clear plastic bottle with a swan-shaped neck. Larkin suspected it was originally designed to water tiny plants. "Untampered with." Camryn opened the bottle and shook it over her hand. "Empty."

She put the bottle down. "Wait," Larkin said. "It's in the wrong place."

"No, it isn't," Camryn said.

Larkin picked up the bottle. "It says—"

The handwriting, underneath the bottle, read *Juliet's sleeping poison.*

"Yeah," Camryn said, "Rebecca wrote it wrong. Everyone knows what it means, though."

Larkin also knew what it meant—not just because Rebecca had written *poison* instead of *potion,* but also because of the way she'd written *Juliet.* The loop on the bottom of the *J.*

Larkin had seen that loop before—and everyone would know what it meant, soon enough.

Which meant she had to find Rebecca as quickly as possible.

CHAPTER 20

"Sixty minutes until curtain." It was Velvet, omniscient and omnipotent, her voice in every speaker. From this point on, she would keep time—and if the clocks said there were fifty-nine minutes until curtain and Velvet said there were sixty, her call would be the one that counted.

"Thank you, sixty."

Larkin said the words, along with the rest of the company, as she texted Ed.

Going to Mess Hall to find Rebecca.

If you see her before I do, keep her with you.

If you don't see me in the next fifteen minutes, come find me.

"Stage left props table clear," Camryn said.

"Stage left props table clear," Beatrix repeated.

"Thirty minutes until house opens."

"Thank you, thirty."

Larkin put her phone in her pocket. She crossed stage right, along with Camryn, dodging the college students who were sweeping the proscenium. She was about to take the downstage right stairs, exiting the stage and entering the house, when Camryn stopped her.

"I'm going to need that phone," the assistant stage manager said, holding out her cardboard box, "and I'm going to need to watch you turn it off."

Camryn was almost apologetic—she was addressing the artistic director, after all—but at this point in the production the hierarchy had flipped. The tech crew, led by the stage manager and enforced by the assistant stage manager, were technically in charge—which meant that Camryn outranked Larkin, and both of them knew it.

So Larkin turned off her burner phone and tossed it into the box.

Then she thanked Camryn.

Then she left the stage and began climbing the house right stairs.

Larkin kept her neck free and her shoulders back—she knew just enough Alexander Technique to handle that—and carried herself as calmly as possible. She had to leave the amphitheater and navigate the beaten-down path to the mess hall without attracting anyone's attention. She kept her focus soft, knowing that the sightline rules applied nearly as well offstage as on. The best way to remain unseen was to avoid catching anybody's eyes. If Larkin let herself look at any specific person, they'd look back—which meant she could not confirm whether Clarissa Bankshaw Morris was still in the amphitheater, or whether Farah still had her socks pulled up over her ankle bracelet, or whether Jay was watching her leave.

Then she was out of the theater and into what would have been the lobby if it had been indoors. Larkin let her mind, not her eyes, observe the people queuing and clustering around the box office and the bar—*Will Call* and *Last Call*, respectively—and avoided direct contact with anyone who might want to interact with the Artistic Director.

She turned, walking directly underneath a vendor tent, Coffee Shop espresso on her right and Juliet Fans on her left. The same *J*, with the loop. Someone must have gotten Rebecca to make the sign, after Preview Night. After Larkin had sent Portia onstage with the same fan, turning the cheap piece of swag into that summer's must-have accessory. After they had found Amelia's body, in the cabin Larkin and Rebecca and Ed and Beatrix had shared, with a dagger in her breast and a note in her hand.

I did it. I wanted to play Juliet. I'm sorry.

The looped *J*, the curve at the end of the *t*.

Someone must have gotten Rebecca to write that, too.

Which was why Larkin had to find Rebecca before anyone got her to do anything else—or before anyone caught on to what she'd done.

———

"Rebecca!" Larkin called out, keeping her voice bright. She had never been to the mess hall this late in the evening. She wasn't expecting the sun, just at the top of the treeline, to shine spots into her eyes. Larkin blinked, trying to clear her vision. Now was the time to look, after all—and all she could see was two dark afterimages of the sun before twilight. "Rebecca? Are you here? I need to talk to you."

"She's not here." It was Peg. Her voice sounded lower than it ought to be. Larkin stumbled forward until she was close enough to see the bits of Peg that weren't obscured by sunspot and shadow. The lighting designer, with her utility belt and her utilitarian haircut, leaning awkwardly against a picnic table. One hand gripping the metal pole that looped the benches in place, as if to hold herself together.

"Do you know where she is?" Larkin crouched down. Something about Peg didn't look right. She blinked again. There were dark spots in her eyes and dark spots on Peg's shirt and something, in the center, that she couldn't quite see. "I need to talk to her."

"I already talked to her," Peg said. "She told me everything."

Larkin blinked again. A dagger—no, a kitchen knife, the kind with the wooden handle and the two little metal circles holding it in place—embedded in Peg's shoulder.

"She confessed?" Larkin asked.

"Yes," Peg said. "And then she stabbed me."

CHAPTER 21

"Forty-five minutes until curtain." There were speakers, somewhere, in the mess hall. Larkin hadn't known that. There was so much she hadn't known—hadn't understood, anyway—and so much that still didn't make sense.

"Thank you, forty-five," Peg said. Then she smiled, grimly, at Larkin. "It's a good thing they don't need me to do the show, right?"

"We need you!" Larkin said. If Peg was asking permission to die, Larkin wasn't granting it. "You've just got to hold on until I can find a phone." She stood up, wondering whether it would be quicker to find Ed or figure out how to reinstall the landline in the kitchen. "Don't move."

"Don't worry," Peg said. "I'm not going anywhere."

"Great," Larkin said. "Then I'm going to go get help."

"Wait," Peg said. "First you need to find Rebecca."

"But you've been stabbed," Larkin said. The spots in front of her eyes were beginning to fade; the spots on Peg's faded T-shirt were beginning to darken. "She stabbed you."

"Not critically," Peg said. "She asked me, before she did it, whether anyone had ever died of being stabbed in the shoulder." Peg shifted position and winced. "I decided not to tell her about gangrene."

"So you're not worried—"

"Of course not," Peg said. "I'll probably need some stitching up, and I definitely don't want to move until we can get a medical professional to pull the blade out, but I told her to use a clean knife and stab me in the fat part and everything would be all right." She forced out another smile. "That girl almost used a serrated knife. Thank goodness I stopped her."

"But you didn't stop her from stabbing you."

"She told me it was her only option," Peg said. "I mean, I don't think she thought it was true, I'm sure she considered plenty of options, but this was the one she picked." She looked up at Larkin. "And here I am, and here you are, and maybe this was what she wanted to happen."

Larkin sat on the picnic table. She looked, as far as she could, in every direction. No sign of Rebecca. No sign of Ed, who had to know that Larkin had just passed the fifteen-minute mark. She sighed. "Okay. If this is what Rebecca wanted to happen, then *why*?"

"Because you and I are the only adults in the company who care about her," Peg said. "We're the only people she can trust."

Larkin considered this. "Her parents—"

"Care for her," Peg said, "but don't care about her."

Larkin knew this was true. Clarissa and Manny valued Rebecca exactly as much as she could help them achieve their goals. Which meant—

"She did it for them, didn't she," Larkin said. "All of it."

"That's what she told me," Peg said. "She poisoned Tyler. She stabbed Amelia. She wanted to destroy the show that had destroyed her family."

Something about this didn't make sense. "Why did Rebecca frame Amelia for Tyler's death?"

"I don't know," Peg said. "Maybe because she thought that would be the easiest way to get away with it."

"But you figured it out," Larkin said. "You saw Rebecca's handwriting on Amelia's suicide note."

"I never saw the note," Peg said, "and I didn't figure anything out." She laughed, and a tiny bit of blood appeared at the edge of her stab wound. "I'm not a detective, like you. All I did was walk with Rebecca to the mess hall, to get that garbage bag she wanted. She was all smiles, all happy, the way a kid should be, you know?"

"The way she's never really been," Larkin said, "until tonight."

"And then she got some kind of message on this phone she was carrying," Peg said. "It was this tiny phone, cheap little thing. She had hidden it in her shoe, if you can believe it. Tucked it right in the side."

Larkin could believe it. *User Nine,* she thought. She wondered how Rebecca had gotten internet access before the rest of them—and how long she'd had it, and who else knew that she could send and receive messages.

"So she reads her text, or whatever it was," Peg said, "and then everything changes. She starts shaking, and she tells me that I have to sit down and pay attention, because she needs to confess to being a murderer, and then she needs to make it look like she tried to murder me."

"And you agreed to this?"

"Honestly," Peg said, "it seemed like the best move."

Larkin thought about everything she knew about Peg. How kind she was to everyone. How careful she was with her own resources, to ensure that she always had something to share with anyone who asked. If there were anyone who would listen to a teenage girl's confession and then advise her on the best way to fake a fatal wound, it would be the stalwart, stabworthy Peg. Larkin didn't even want to think about what might have happened if Isabella had gone to the mess hall with Rebecca. More screaming, probably. More blood. A serrated knife instead of a clean blade. Everything would have gone wrong.

But something—even if it didn't make sense yet—had gone right. For Larkin, for Peg, for Rebecca, and for the person who had sent Rebecca that message on her tiny, secret phone.

Which meant—

"This entire thing is a distraction," Larkin said. "Rebecca didn't murder anybody."

"How do you know?"

"Because—"

They both heard the footsteps at the same time. Fast, loud, the kind of person who didn't care who heard them coming. Larkin looked up—and there was Ed, running full-speed down the path, his own burner phone in his hand.

"We've got to get to Farah," he said. "Her heartrate just skyrocketed."

CHAPTER 22

"Where is she?" Larkin asked—even though she was pretty sure she already knew. This murderer liked to repeat things, after all.

"Equity cabin," Ed said—which was exactly what Larkin was expecting to hear. Rebecca had also been lured to her cabin, a place in which she felt safe, before she had been asked to write Amelia's suicide note.

But Farah's death—Larkin suspected—was not going to be so carefully staged.

"Call Jay," Larkin said. This was not what Ed was expecting to hear—but his eyes, focused on Larkin, hadn't yet registered Peg's injury. She doubted he even knew the lighting designer was there. "Tell him to come to the mess hall. Tell him there's a first-aid kit hanging on the wall next to the refrigerator. Above the fire extinguisher."

Ed held up his burner phone. "I don't have Jay's number in my contacts."

"Call Elliott, then," Larkin said. "He'll know how to reach Jay."

Ed looked down at his phone—but his eyes caught on

the knife sticking out of Peg's shoulder. "What happened?"

"She'll explain it to you," Larkin said. "Stay with her until Jay arrives. Then come find me."

She turned—and ran—towards the Equity cabin.

Larkin hoped that Ed and Peg could figure out, on their own, that a lead surgical resident would be more than capable of assessing and treating Peg's stab wound. She hoped that Jay could live up to his capabilities—but he had to, that was his deal, the angel on his shoulder would respond to the knife in Peg's—and that she hadn't just left her boyfriend and her lighting designer to the enmities of her enemy.

But that was a problem for them to solve.

She had to save Farah.

The Equity cabin was lit, from the inside; the door bumped, when Larkin opened it, against Farah's foot. The sock, pulled up over her ankle bracelet. The body, limp on the floor. The bottle that had once held her sleeping potion —the smaller one—was now held in the cradle of her open hand.

Larkin bent down. "Farah," she said.

The actress's dark skin was still warm. It almost felt— and Larkin really wished she had taken a first-aid certification before accepting this job—like she still had a pulse.

"Farah," Larkin said again. How long did it take someone to die of cyanide poisoning? She looked around the cabin, looking for anything she could use as an anti- dote—but she didn't think aspirin was the right choice, and she didn't see any ipecac, and she was pretty sure an enormous bottle of water wouldn't solve the problem.

"Hello?" Larkin called out. "Is anyone else here? Can somebody help?" She lifted her eyes towards the bunk that had once been Juliet's balcony. "If there's any God—"

"Five minutes until house opens."

The Equity cabin, which had electricity, also had speakers.

"Thank you, five," Farah said.

She was still alive—and Larkin was by her side, helping her sit up, stroking the streaks of gold in her blue-black hair.

"My mother believes there is a God," Farah said, "and our stories are already written."

"My friend Anni says there's a mathematical equivalent to God," Larkin said, "and although the equations that determine the universe can't be changed, we can change ourselves."

"We are not a play, then," Farah said.

"Nope," Larkin said. "We are a problem, in the process of being solved."

Farah considered this. "We solved this problem, too," she said, turning her face towards Larkin. There was someone else on the other side of her *we*. Someone who had changed everything. "We rehearsed it."

Larkin kept one hand on Farah's hair. The other on her shoulder, feeling the heartbeat in her neck. Steady, a little fast—was that good or bad? "Rehearsed what?" It was probably good to keep Farah talking.

"The death scene," Farah said. "Portia and I blocked the whole thing, at your friends' mansion." She looked at the bottle in her hand. "It was her idea."

"What idea?"

"To know how a person would die of cyanide poisoning," Farah said. "What happens to the body, in what order." She set the bottle down, on the floor. "Rapid breathing is first."

Farah began to breathe, rapidly, in Larkin's arms.

Larkin gripped Farah's shoulder, out of fear, until both of them relaxed.

"I probably shouldn't do it again," Farah said, letting her breath slow. "It was terrifying enough to do it the first time. But it started like that." She still sounded like she was in shock, even though Larkin didn't really know what shock sounded like. She'd only ever read about it, in books —or seen it on the stage.

"You also have to get your heartbeat up," Farah said. "So high that your face turns red." She smiled at Larkin. "Portia and I worked on that. We couldn't ever get it high enough to change the color of my skin." She let her fingers flutter against her cheek. "But we knew that most white people don't know anything about how brown people blush, so we left it alone."

Larkin was starting to understand. "You practiced faking your own death."

"Until it was perfect," Farah said. "We didn't tell anybody, either. Your friend Ben thought we were doing each other's hair."

Larkin remembered Ben saying this. "You wanted to be prepared, in case anybody tried to poison you."

"Yes," Farah said. "Which meant we also had to practice taking the drink, without letting any of the liquid touch my lips or enter my mouth, and then faking the swallow."

Larkin looked at the bottle. "Because somebody wanted you to drink that," she said.

"Yes," Farah said, "and if I hadn't, she would have tried to kill me in another way." Her heartbeat increased, just slightly. "She had a gun." Slowly, carefully, every word a memory. "I had to fake my own death so she wouldn't use the gun. Thank God I knew how."

"Thirty minutes until curtain," their god said, through their speakers. "House is opening."

That was when Ed opened the door.

"Farah—" he said.

"I'm fine," Farah said.

"Peg?" Larkin asked.

"She's fine," Ed said. "Jay and Anni and Elliott are all with her."

"I almost got murdered," Farah said, reaching her hand out to the bunkbed ladder. Pulling herself up. Pulling herself together. "But Portia showed me how to fake my death." She smiled at Ed. "She also kissed me."

"I was hoping she would," Ed said, smiling. He'd known about this. He'd probably helped instigate it. That must have been what he and Portia had been whispering about, all summer long. "You can tell us about it later. Right now, we've got to get you stable."

"We also need to find the person who did this to you," Larkin said. "The murderer." She looked at Farah—who looked at the floor, at the bottle, at the bunk. At Ed, as if he might still be able to help her; at her hands, as if she knew he could not.

"You know who it is, right?" Larkin asked.

Farah nodded.

"But you don't want to say."

Farah shook her head.

"Is it Rebecca?" Larkin asked. "She already confessed to poisoning Tyler and stabbing Amelia." That was the part that hadn't made sense—the piece that Larkin hadn't fully put together until she heard herself repeating Peg's words. Amelia had been poisoned first and stabbed afterwards—and Rebecca hadn't known that.

"The police are going to arrest Rebecca, if you say it's her," Larkin continued, hoping Farah would understand that saving a young girl could be just as important as protecting herself. "There's evidence everywhere. Handwriting. Probably fingerprints."

Farah looked at Ed again. She wanted to nod—Larkin knew it—but she would not.

"I can't say," she said.

"Yes, you can."

It was Rebecca.

She'd hidden herself in the Equity cabin bathroom.

She'd also been crying.

"You have to say it was me," she said. "It only works if you say it was me."

Larkin watched the seventeen-year-old girl, her hair pulled back under its bandana, her hands stained with Peg's blood, take her place at the center of the room.

"I did it," Rebecca said. "Say I did it."

"But you didn't," Larkin said.

"I murdered Tyler, I murdered Amelia, I attempted to murder Peg, and I attempted to murder you," Rebecca said. She was looking at Farah. She would not look at Larkin.

"But you didn't," Farah repeated.

"But neither of us can say who did," Rebecca said, "and if you say it was me, I get tried as a minor." She finally met Larkin's eyes. "That's what the murderer wants."

CHAPTER 23

arkin looked at Rebecca. Sweat on the edge of her bandana. Snot swiped across her right cheek. Blood on both of her hands.

"The murderer wants you to be tried as a minor?"

Rebecca nodded. "That's what has to happen."

Nothing about this made sense. "So you're going to lie under oath?"

"No," Rebecca said. "I'm just going to plead guilty. That's all you have to do. Then the lawyers plea bargain, or something." She looked at Larkin, trying to get her to understand. "We have very good lawyers."

Larkin asked herself who was on the other side of Rebecca's *we*—and then she knew.

She also knew what she needed to do next.

"Ed-hay," Larkin said. "Ext-tay Elliott-hay and-hay ask-hay im-hay oo-tay ing-bray aire-Clay oo-tay amp-cay." She didn't know Morse Code, but she did know Pig Latin. She hoped Ed did, too.

"*Je vais*," Ed said. Larkin knew just enough French to know he wasn't talking about vegetables. She saw him take out his burner phone—and she saw Rebecca's eyes turn immediately towards the flicker of light in Ed's hand. She had to distract Rebecca, fast.

"How did you get access to the internet?" Larkin asked. "You had it the whole time, didn't you."

"Not the whole time," Rebecca said. "It took me, like, three days."

"To get the password?"

"No," Rebecca said. "I got that the first day." She smiled, the way Larkin had seen her smile when she was joking with Camryn. A teenage-girl smile, hesitant and powerful at the same time. "I watched Beatrix log into the network. She put the password in her phone. Then she turned it from dots to letters, to make sure she'd gotten it right. I saw the reflection in her glasses."

Larkin nodded. "And the other two days?"

"I had to wait for Beatrix to leave her phone unattended," Rebecca said, "so I could use it to give myself access to the network."

"On your burner phone," Larkin said. "Not your real one."

"This *is* my real phone," Rebecca said, pulling the tiny device out of her shoe. "Everyone in my class has one. It's the only way we can talk to each other without our parents listening in."

Larkin knew Rebecca meant *text* instead of *talk* and *read* instead of *listen*. By the time the seventeen-year-old had completed her sentence—for double murder, and double attempted murder—the terms might have switched places completely, the way *literally* and *figuratively* had. Or they might be using something completely different to communicate. Biometrics, probably. Pen and paper, for the people who refused the matrix. Either way, Rebecca would emerge into a world that had no place for her.

Which, to be fair, was a bit like the world she'd been living in for the past four weeks.

It was also like—

"So when Ed and I heard you texting by the lake that one day," Larkin said, giving Rebecca a question to answer while she processed her thoughts, "you were just texting your friends."

Rebecca nodded. "It's, like, the only place where anyone can have any privacy. Except for the toilets, which are gross."

Larkin nodded, replicating Rebecca's movements as she put the last pieces of the puzzle in place. That day, by the lake—she and Ed had been asking themselves *who had money*.

The Bankshaws and the Emersons.

"Farah," Larkin asked, "what does your father do?" She remembered Farah saying *accountant*. She didn't remember which kind.

"He's a forensic accountant," Farah said.

"What does that mean?" Larkin asked. She knew what *forensic* meant, and she knew what *accountant* meant, but she wasn't precisely sure how they fit together.

"It means that he investigates financial crimes."

"Rebecca," Larkin asked, "is your family under investigation?"

Rebecca looked at the blood on her hands. She looked at the bottle, potioned and poisoned, next to Farah. "Do you even read the news?" she said, her scoff failing her as her feet scuffed the floor.

"No," Larkin said. "But it doesn't matter. I've figured it out."

She turned to Ed. "Ell-tay Elliott-hay oo-tay ell-tay aire-Clay oo-tay etain-day arrisa-Clay ankshaw-Bay orris-May."

"No," Rebecca said. Somebody must have taught her Pig Latin at some point. Her father, maybe. "You can't."

"Yes," Larkin said. "I can—because it's what your mother wants."

"How do you know?"

"Because she told you to pretend to stab Peg," Larkin said, "to ensure you'd have an alibi while she committed her third murder."

That was when the door opened.

"Fourth murder," Clarissa Bankshaw Morris said, entering the Equity cabin. She was holding a tiny silver gun; it wavered, for just a moment, before she was able to aim it at Farah's head. "Or fourth attempted murder. Does it count if you attempt to murder someone more than once? Does it count if they trick you into thinking they're dead?" She laughed. It was a rich, middle-age-woman laugh, anxious and victorious at the same time. "I suppose it doesn't matter. I'll be fine, either way."

She cocked the gun. "And so will my family."

CHAPTER 24

"Fifteen minutes until curtain," Velvet said, from the speakers. "Ten minutes until places for act 1, scene 1."

"Thank you, fifteen," Larkin said. "Thank you, ten." Then she took her place at the center of the room. "By the time the curtain rises, Clarissa Bankshaw Morris will be under arrest for the murders of Tyler Mackintosh and Amelia Jorgensen."

"And Farah Emerson," Clarissa said. She took a step closer to Farah, adjusting her shooting arm. "She's the only murder that matters."

"Was that really the best way to prevent the Emerson family from investigating the Bankshaw family?" Larkin asked, taking a close look at the tip of Clarissa's gun. She was nearly certain she'd seen that gun before—and even more certain that Clarissa hadn't. "By threatening to eliminate their daughter?" Larkin shook her head. "You have to ask yourself what you'd do if they called your bluff."

"We did," Clarissa said. "We all did." She looked at

Larkin, finding her eyes and losing her aim. "This was always part of the plan."

"But you changed the plan," Larkin said. "That was where things started to go wrong."

"You kept changing the bottles!" Clarissa said, swinging her gun hand towards Larkin. "And you—" She turned, swerving, towards her daughter. "You told me Juliet poisoned herself." Clarissa laughed, again. More anxious, this time. Less certain of victory. "I let my child spend an entire summer working on a production of *Romeo and Juliet* and she still can't keep track of who gets poisoned and who gets stabbed."

"Daddy played Romeo four times and you didn't keep track," Rebecca said. "It's confusing." She considered this. "No, it's like Shakespeare distracts us, so we forget what's about to happen. I think he did it on purpose."

"He does," Larkin said. "I mean, he did." She suddenly had everyone's attention. "It's kind of the magic of the play, the way nobody knows how it ends even though everybody knows how it ends."

Ed smiled at her. Then he looked at his phone, which was flickering with notifications. *"Je devrais leur demander d'amener Claire à la cabine, n'est-ce pas?"*

Larkin only understood two of those words, but that was enough. "Ess-yay," she said, keeping her focus on the three women in front of her. "You put the cyanide in the bottle that Rebecca had incorrectly labeled *Juliet's sleeping poison*," she said to Clarissa. "That was your first attempted murder."

"I suppose it would have been," Clarissa said, "if we're keeping track."

"And Farah would have died if Susan and Stanley hadn't insisted I swap the bottle for something that would fit in her girdle," Larkin said, "and if you—" She looked at

Rebecca. "You knew the smaller bottle was poisoned, didn't you. That's why the bottles were switched, again, right before the final dress rehearsal. You did that because you wanted Farah to live."

"Don't say anything about what you knew," Clarissa said, to her daughter, "not without a lawyer present."

"Fine," Larkin said. "If Rebecca can't talk, then I'll keep talking." She looked, directly, at Clarissa. "You saw Farah walk onstage, during the final dress rehearsal, and drink from a bottle you weren't expecting. A bottle you hadn't poisoned."

"It should have killed her," Clarissa said. "Everything would have been easier if it had just killed her." She shifted the gun away from Larkin and towards Farah. "I should kill her now."

"You can't," Larkin said. "Not yet." *What does Clarissa want?* "Not until your daughter understands everything that happened next."

"I understand enough of it," Rebecca said. "When Mom realized that her plan hadn't worked, she went backstage and found the bottle that Romeo uses at the end of the play." She looked at her mother. "But you weren't sure, either, who got poisoned and who got stabbed. So you took the real dagger, the one that ends up on the props table after Juliet removes it in act 4, scene 3, and swapped it for the fake dagger." The implications were obvious, even though it took Rebecca a second to put them together. "You were prepared to kill two people."

"I was prepared to kill as many people as it took," Clarissa said, "as long as Farah died."

"But you weren't prepared to go to prison," Larkin said. Clarissa's head twisted, quickly, towards Larkin's direction. "That was the real plan, wasn't it. You were the disposable Bankshaw. The one who didn't have a job. The one who could go to prison for a few years, maybe even twenty years if your lawyers weren't as good as you thought they were, and come out ready to live off your family's collected wealth for the rest of your days."

"It was my mother's idea," Clarissa said. "She told me that the purpose of prison wasn't to incarcerate. It wasn't even to rehabilitate. It was to make people poor."

Ed looked up from his phone. "She's right," he said, "which is why there are two groups of people who aren't deterred by the possibility of imprisonment."

"Those who are already poor," Clarissa said, "and those who are already rich."

"Extremely poor and extremely rich," Ed corrected. "The people who understand that their financial situation won't change, no matter what happens. Some people even believe that going to prison is the safer choice. Three hots and a cot, if you're poor." He looked at Clarissa. "The opportunity to wait out a family scandal, if you're rich."

"But you didn't want to wait," Larkin said. "You wanted to send Rebecca, instead."

"She would have been tried as a minor," Clarissa said. "It would have been a shorter prison term. We would have been able to frame the story around Manny and our divorce. A depressed, privileged teen taking revenge on the festival that destroyed her family." She looked at Rebecca. "You would have been okay."

"And it would have taken the heat off your brother and his investment algorithm," Larkin said. "Or whatever it was that Farah's father was investigating."

She looked at Farah, who shook her head.

"I had no idea any of this was going on," Farah said. "My dad never tells me about his cases." She looked confused. "Did my mother know? Did they allow me to participate in this Shakespeare Festival even though it was full of people who were threatening to kill me if my dad didn't back off?"

"No," Ed said. His voice was calming. Sincere. Trustworthy. "Your parents couldn't have known." Larkin knew he was making a lucky guess. "Manny had been fired as Artistic Director several months before you auditioned."

"And my soon-to-be ex-husband never uses the Bankshaw name," Clarissa said.

"Daddy says they're not his family," Rebecca said. "He says that whenever Grandma Bankshaw looks at him, he can hear her thinking all the words you aren't supposed to say about Jewish people."

"When he tells that story at dinner parties," Clarissa says, "he lists the words—and then he ends the list with *actor*."

Farah, unbelievably, laughed. "My mother does something similar," she said. "Except she uses different words, and she ends her list with *survivor*."

"I almost wish I didn't have to kill you," Clarissa said.

"Of course you wish you didn't," Larkin said, wondering how long it would be before Clarissa got up the nerve to fire her gun. Hoping Officer Claire Novak would arrive before Clarissa realized what kind of gun she was holding. "You never wanted to kill Farah. You were just doing it because your family said you had to." She looked, closely, at Clarissa Bankshaw Morris. "But you wanted to kill Amelia Jorgensen."

"Killing Amelia was a necessary evil," Clarissa said. "We had just learned that Farah's father didn't have as much evidence as he thought he did, and we needed a way to draw attention away from the family."

"So you decided to murder an innocent girl," Larkin said.

"She wasn't that innocent," Clarissa said, "and she

wasn't a girl. Amelia was a full-grown woman." She looked at her not-quite-grown daughter. "She was also the prime suspect. Rebecca told me."

"I read your letter," Rebecca said, turning to Larkin before looking at her shoes. "The one you wrote your friend. You left it on the bunk."

"It's okay," Larkin said, trying to remember which letter Rebecca meant. She had written Anni a lot of letters, over the past four weeks. "It was probably in plain sight. That means it's not a crime." She turned back to Clarissa. "So you poisoned Amelia, dragged her body to our cabin, and staged a suicide."

"Yes," Clarissa said.

"With a confession note," Larkin continued, "that you got Rebecca to write."

"Yes," Clarissa said again.

"As insurance," Larkin concluded, "just in case the police figured out that Amelia didn't actually kill herself."

"Rebecca had agreed to all of this," Clarissa said. "She knew what could happen to all of us if she didn't."

"Fun fact," Ed said—and Larkin knew, once again, that he was guessing—"minors can't technically make those kinds of agreements."

"That's true," Larkin said, watching Rebecca's face. By the time Rebecca would be old enough to know whether or not they'd gotten it wrong, she'd also be old enough to understand why they'd wanted her to think they were right. "Anyone who isn't eighteen can't enter into any kind of binding contract or conspiracy or anything like that. The law automatically assumes they've been pressured into it." Larkin looked carefully at Rebecca. "That's contract law, not criminal law, so you may still get in trouble. You may even have to plead guilty if it turns out you did something illegal." She held Rebecca's dazed gaze.

"But don't let yourself *feel* guilty. That's a distraction. Remember that this was not your fault."

Rebecca nodded—hesitantly, and then powerfully. "I told Mom I wouldn't do the dagger part," she said. "I said she had to."

And Clarissa hadn't known, Larkin thought, *that she put the dagger in the wrong part of the body. She still doesn't know that she's holding the wrong kind of gun.*

"There's just one part I still don't understand," Ed said, his eyes meeting Larkin's, his phone flashing in his hand. They were almost through with all of this, as long as they could keep everyone talking until Claire arrived. "Why ask Rebecca to stab Peg?"

"Yeah, Mom, why?" Now Rebecca looked even more powerful. "And how did you get my secret phone number?"

"I've known about your secret phone since you bought it," Clarissa said. "You do realize I keep track of your bank statements, right?" She sighed. "If you had just turned on your smartphone, like everyone else, I would have been able to use the tracking system to find you. I would have been able to tell you to make sure you had an alibi for the rest of the evening."

"Because," Larkin said, "your mother loves you, after all." She looked at Clarissa. "You changed your mind about letting Rebecca take the fall."

Clarissa nodded. "I did."

"You wanted to make sure she was accounted for."

"I did."

"So you asked her to stab Peg."

"No," Clarissa said. "I told her to stay with Peg." She looked at her daughter. "You stabbed someone?"

Rebecca showed her mother her phone screen. "Mom. It says *stab*."

That was when Clarissa started crying. The kind of tears Larkin had never seen in real life, only in Shakespearean and Greek tragedies. They watched, in silence, as Clarissa Bankshaw Morris dropped to her knees. Rested her forehead against the floor. Placed her gun—*she still didn't know about the gun*—against her temple.

"Everyone stay back," Clarissa said. "Rebecca, I'm sorry. You know I love you."

She put her finger against the trigger.

She paused.

"Tell my family to call off the feud."

Then she pulled.

CHAPTER 25

The gun—as Rebecca and Larkin had both known it wouldn't—didn't go off.

Clarissa Bankshaw Morris pulled the trigger a second time.

Click.

"Mom," Rebecca said. "It's a prop gun."

"Places for act 1, scene 1."

"Thank you, places."

"It's a prop gun?"

"Yeah," Rebecca said. "I mean, I should know. That gun definitely came from the props shed."

"What does that mean?" Clarissa looked at the gun in her hand. She looked at her purse, on the floor. She tried to connect the two events. "How did I end up with a prop gun?"

"I swapped it," Manny Morris said, from the doorway. He entered the cabin, dressed as Romeo—followed by Claire, dressed as Officer Novak.

"Does everyone in your family just, like, wait behind doors until you hear a good entrance line?" Larkin asked.

She still wasn't sure whether she liked Manny, but she was sure glad to see him.

"She's not my family," Manny said, turning away from Clarissa as Officer Novak approached her. "But she—"

Everyone watched as he scooped up Rebecca and held her close.

"This girl is my child."

He kissed his daughter's forehead. "Thanks for telling me that your mother had a gun. And for telling me where I could find a nearly identical one." He looked at Officer Novak. "I assume this doesn't make me an accessory or anything like that. I mean, I swapped the gun so she *couldn't* murder anybody."

Claire snapped Clarissa's handcuffs in place. "I'm going to need to bring all of you in for questioning," she said. Then she winked at Larkin. "In just about four hours."

"You mean—" Larkin couldn't believe it.

"I've heard it said," Claire said, grinning, "that the show must go on." She looked at Manny. "You'd better get a move on. Romeo's right at the beginning of the play." She looked at Farah. "I think you still have a few scenes to get yourself ready."

"Isn't this going to cause trouble," Ed asked, "at the police station?"

"Trust me," Claire said, "there are going to be at least four hours of interrogation and paperwork with this one" —she gestured towards Clarissa—"and this one"—she glanced at Rebecca—"before I can even begin to get started with the rest of you." She looked at Clarissa. "I assume neither of you will say anything without a lawyer present?" Clarissa shook her head. "Make it six hours, then," Claire said, giving Larkin another wink. "Go break a leg."

Manny nodded, already two steps closer to the door. Then he turned back, taking one step towards his daughter. "Are you going to be all right on your own?"

Rebecca, who was holding out her wrists as Claire applied zip-tie handcuffs, blinked back her tears, and sniffed back her snot. "Yes." It was obvious to everyone in the room that she was lying. Protecting her parents, one last time. "Go be Romeo."

Manny shook his head. "No. I'm going with you." He looked at Claire. "I can stay with Rebecca, right?"

"If you want to sit in the police station lobby while we take her in," Claire said, "that's fine by me."

Manny reached out to Rebecca. He put his hand between her two cuffed ones. "I'll be right on the other side of the door," he said. Then he turned to Larkin. "I'm sorry about the show."

"It's all right," Larkin said. It actually was, watching Manny Morris act like a man instead of an actor. It felt like the end of a story. "I'll go give a speech or something. Get all of those tickets refunded."

"I don't think you'll have to," Farah said. She held up her phone, showing Larkin what Caleb Alderton had just posted to social media.

About to go onstage as Romeo. I wonder who will play Juliet this time.

Larkin looked at the message—which included a photo of Caleb in doublet and hose, an ad-hoc costume courtesy of SuStan—and then looked at Ed.

"Did you have anything to do with this?"

"If you're asking me whether I was able to get in touch with Caleb before his bus made its first stop, and whether I was able to convince Ben and Mitchell to drive to the bus stop and bring our understudy back," Ed said, "then you already know the answer."

Larkin leapt up, crossed the room, and threw her arms around the man she loved. "Thank you," she said, letting her long dark hair fall onto Ed's strong dark shoulder.

"It's what I do," Ed said.

Then he kissed her.

Then she kissed him.

"And. . . scene," Larkin whispered, into Ed's ear.

CHAPTER 26

"We are gathered here today," Larkin said, "to bid farewell to a beloved companion."

The six of them—Larkin, Ed, Anni, Elliott, Josephine, and Claire—stood side by side. Larkin wore black. Claire wore black. Anni wore two barrettes shaped like dog biscuits. They might actually have been dog biscuits, at one point. Larkin would have to ask Anni later.

Right now, she had to perform a funeral service.

"We will begin with some original poetry, written and read by Dr. Josephine Day."

Her mother stepped forward.

I cannot write what lies beyond this life
And simultaneously speak the truth
But if one remains sensate after death
I hope you sense we're thinking about you.

Josephine looked, embarrassedly, at the paper in her hand. "I think I'm a better teacher than I am a poet." She turned to Larkin. "You should have let me read the Neruda."

"Nope," Larkin said. "Only original work." She turned to Ed. "Are you ready?"

"Absolutely," Ed said. He looked at Anni. "Shall we?"

"A song," Larkin intoned, "written by Dr. Ed Jackson and performed with accompaniment by Anni Morgan."

Ed sang, his tenor crisp against the clear July morning, as Anni blew into a melodica.

Unleash this spirit
So the Lord can fetch it
And St. Peter can pet it
And let it sleep on Heaven's bed
Unleash this spirit
And let it play
In the great green fields
And the great blue lakes
And the great gold streets
Where the angels meet
Until the day
When Christ comes down and commands us all to stay.

"I know it's doggerel," he said, smiling at Larkin. "Pun intended."

This was the second funeral Larkin had ever attended. The first one she had ever officiated. So far, the services had been fairly similar—words, music, jokes—but she was pretty sure that most funerals didn't include close-up magic.

"An original illusion," Larkin said, "created by Elliott Fox."

Elliott's performance was simple and silent. A standard deck of cards; a fifty-third card bearing a familiar face. It appeared, reappeared, disappeared. He gestured towards Claire's pocket. She pulled out the handmade card and held it to her chest.

"Thank you," she said.

"Ashes to ashes," Larkin said, picking up the small box that contained the cremains, "and dust to dust." She turned towards Claire. "Is there anything else that needs to be said?"

"Pal," Claire said, taking the box and placing it in the freshly dug hole next to the rosebush, "you were a very good dog."

———

Anni and Elliott had offered to host the luncheon—and so two cars and two bicycles traveled the three miles that separated Pratincola, Iowa from the Morgan-Fox farmhouse.

"It was built in 1859," Anni said, taking them into the front room. "That's pre-Civil War."

"The floors are mostly original," Elliott said, inviting them to bend down and touch the freshly varnished wood. "The crown moulding was added in the early 1900s, I believe."

"All of the front windows are leaded glass," Anni said. "You probably shouldn't lick them."

"I wasn't planning to," Larkin said. Then she squeezed Ed's hand. "Unless-hay e-thay only-hay ing-thay or-fay unch-lay is-hay occoli-bray ig-fay izza-pay," she whispered, into his ear. They'd learn Morse Code later.

"Why did nobody else want to buy this place?" Josephine asked. "It's beautiful."

"But it isn't turnkey," Elliott said. "Anni and I are going to have to spend at least a year shoring it up." He took them into what might have been a parlor, in its better days. "All this wallpaper will need to come down."

"And all this carpet," Anni said, scootching her socked foot into the shag, "will need to be ripped up."

"We may also need to update the HVAC," Elliott said, "since all we've got are ceiling fans and radiators."

"Which we can handle," Anni said, "but our piano can't." She turned towards Elliott, her gaze even more intimate than a kiss. "When we get a piano. A real one."

"Next year," Elliott said. "First we prepare the house for winter—"

"And then we prepare the garden for spring."

A timer—one of the old-fashioned ones, with a dial that turned and a buzz so loud it shook the leaded glass—went off, in the kitchen.

"I should check the bread," Anni said. "It's going to be bread, and cheese, and cold cuts, and cut fruit. I looked up what you were supposed to serve at a funeral, and all of the top results were sponsored advertisements for funeral companies, so I got an etiquette book out of the library instead." She was halfway out the door to the kitchen; she turned around. "It said cold, simple food. Something about hot foods being too hard to digest when you're grieving. I'm not going to wait for the bread to cool, though. We should eat it warm, with butter."

"And coffee!" Larkin called out, as her friend left the room.

"Did you think I would forget your coffee?" Anni called back. "This is the first time we've ever hosted a luncheon in our new home, so I made a list of everything everyone likes! I made a schedule! I'll start heating the water for coffee and tea as soon as I finish tapping the bread with my knuckles to see if it sounds hollow!"

Elliott gestured towards the two-person sofa that used to take up the majority of Anni's tiny apartment. "Claire, Josephine, would you like to sit down?" He turned to Larkin. "We're going to have Anni's family over—officially, not just to walk through the house and open a bottle of bubbly— as soon as we get a little more furniture. I've got some stuff in Champaign-Urbana that we'll have to move, and then we'll probably do some antiquing."

"I'm fine sitting on the floor," Larkin said. "Especially on this beautiful shag carpet." She arranged herself criss-cross applesauce and fingered the fibers. "I notice you didn't provide an historical reference for this stuff. 1970s, maybe?"

"I don't even want to know," Elliott said. He looked towards the kitchen. "Do you need any help in there?"

"No, thank you!" came the response. "Bread is cooling, water is boiling, cheese and fruit and meat are being arranged in alphabetical order!"

"We'll help you move, of course," Ed said, "although I believe the standard payment is a case of beer."

Elliott smiled. "We've got something even better in mind."

———

The *something better* turned out to be an all-expenses-paid cruise.

"A nerd cruise," Larkin said.

"It doesn't have to be a nerd cruise," Anni said, setting the plates on the coffee table that had once taken up the majority of the floorspace in her apartment. "It could just be an ordinary cruise, if you don't want to do the nerd stuff."

"Like what?" Ed asked.

"Tabletop games," Elliott said, "and magic shows. Artificial intelligence demonstrations, seminars about programming and mathematics, music, comedy, sci-fi and fantasy readings, that kind of thing. Plenty of entertainment for all different kinds of nerds."

"Are we nerds?" Larkin asked Ed.

"We are very definitely nerds," Ed said. He turned to Elliott. "What kind of music?"

"Prog rock, prog jazz, prog classical, prog hip-hop," Elliott said. "Plus filk, folk, and the rest of its ilk."

"A lot of people with ukuleles," Anni said, "although you can bring whatever instrument you want. There are concerts and sing-alongs and masterclasses."

"So for me," Ed said, "it could be an all-expenses-paid music cruise."

"Exactly," Elliott said.

"Not quite every expense will be covered, of course," Anni said, "Only the stateroom, the food, the non-premium beverages, the 24-hour game room, and the nearly 24-hour entertainment. You'll still be responsible for the flights, the excursions, the souvenirs, and any premium beverages you choose to purchase."

"What's the difference between a premium and a non-premium beverage?" Ed asked.

"Thirteen dollars, on average," Anni said. "Plus tip."

"Let me rephrase Ed's question," Larkin said. She tried to phrase it in the nerdiest way possible. "What are the *chemical components* of a premium beverage?"

Anni, whose mouth was full of her freshly-baked bread, passed the responsibility of answering to Elliott. "Carbonation, alcohol, or both."

"So coffee is non-premium," Larkin said.

"And so is tea," Ed said. He looked at Larkin. "I don't see any reason to say no."

"I guess we're going on a nerd cruise, then," Larkin said. Anni had spoken about this cruise many times before. She'd gone every year, for over a decade, until the cruise—like everything else—had taken a temporary hiatus. Now it was coming back, and Anni had decided to use her accumulated cruise loyalty points to upgrade her stateroom. This was why she was able to accommodate four guests, all-expenses-paid, without having to pay anything out of pocket beyond taxes and incidentals.

"The suite has a private bedroom, with door," Anni explained, holding out her phone so they could see the photos.

"With door," Claire said, sitting next to Josephine on the sofa.

"With door," Josephine repeated. Their fingers clasped, casually, together. Larkin realized, for the first time, how much her mother and Claire loved each other—and how much both of them loved her.

"There's also a semi-private sleeping area, with blackout curtain," Anni continued. "When the sleeping area is not being used for sleeping, the upper bed folds into the wall and the lower bed folds into a couch."

"I call top bunk," Larkin said, winking at Ed.

"I already called top bunk," Anni said. "You two get the bedroom. Elliott and I get the room with the blackout curtains and the modular beds. Elliott also gets the table, so he can set up his laptop and his chessboards and his decks of cards. I get the space next to the table, which will be just large enough for me to plug in the digital piano."

"Because this is the kind of cruise where people practice the piano," Ed said.

"And their magic, and their writing," Anni said, "and whatever else they might be studying at the time."

"Like *clues*," Claire said, grinning at Larkin.

"I will not be doing any mystery-solving, on this cruise," Larkin said, tossing her long, dark hair. "I will be the only nerd *actually on vacation*."

"The suite also includes a full bath with tub," Elliott said, navigating the conversation back towards general interest, "and a private verandah with four adjustable deck chairs."

"Both of which are accessible from both the main living room and the bedroom," Anni explained, "so the two of you can use the toilet or go out on the verandah without disturbing us."

"And vice versa," Elliott said.

"We've thoroughly considered the logistics," Anni said. "Larkin's on a nine-month contract, so she'll be free for three whole months."

"To take a week-long cruise," Larkin said.

"There's a lot you might want to do before the cruise starts," Anni said. "You could join the online forums and get to know your fellow cruisers, or you could look at the featured guest list and read all of the books written by all of the featured authors." She looked at Claire. "Adamantine Darcy's coming this year."

"Wow," Claire said. "I love her *Time Tangent Gentleman* series."

"I know," Anni said. "I saw you posting about it on social."

"I have every single one of her books," Claire said, "in hardback." She was very close to geeking out. "Except the last one. You know there's only one more left, right? In the *Time Tangent Gentleman* series? Is she going to be writing her last book on the cruise?" Claire looked at Josephine. "Can we go?"

"We have not been invited," Josephine said. "I think this trip is for the young people."

"We're not young," Anni said, "and neither is Adamantine Darcy. She just turned eighty, I believe."

"See?" Claire said, grinning at Josephine. "You won't be the oldest person on the boat."

Anni looked at Larkin. The decision was hers—and it was easy to make.

"Of course you can come," Larkin said. She twitched her nose at her mother. "I bet you'll both love it."

"You'll just have to get your own stateroom," Anni said, finalizing the logistics. Larkin wondered if Anni had already known, when she began the conversation, that it would end with all six of them planning a vacation together. "The interior staterooms are very affordable. No windows, no balcony, but you have the entire rest of the cruise ship to explore if you want to see the ocean."

"I want to see the morgue," Claire said. She grinned at Josephine, again. "Did you know that nearly every cruise ship has a working morgue?"

"The below-deck tour counts as an excursion," Elliott said, "which means it will come with an additional cost." Then he flexed his flexible fingers. "Unless you know somebody who knows how to pick locks."

"Elliott!" Anni said. "You promised the cruise, well over a decade ago, that you would never pick a lock aboard ship again."

"I said I would never pick another lock aboard *that* ship," Elliott said. "This sailing will take place on an entirely different ocean liner."

Larkin watched the two of them begin their dance— back and forth, tumblers falling into position, a lock and a key in perfect harmony. They had picked each other, Anni and Elliott, and they had picked their home. They were able to make choices that Larkin didn't yet feel capable of making. Decisions about the life they wanted to live, even if parts of that life didn't make sense to anyone else. Actions, like buying a house or planting a garden, that would get them there.

Larkin didn't want a farmhouse. She didn't want a

garden. She was pretty sure she didn't want another dog, even though it had never been her dog to begin with and she wouldn't begrudge Claire from finding another pal. Larkin also wasn't sure whether she wanted marriage and children—but she wasn't sure if she wanted marriage without children, and she didn't know what Ed wanted, and she didn't know whether it was the right time to find out. They had only been dating for a year—and by this time next year she might be finishing up her second season with the Summer Shakespeare Festival and he might have a full professorship at Howell College, or she might be working as a barista and he might have to leave Pratincola. Would she ask him to stay? Would he ask her, if she wanted to apply for a directing job somewhere else?

There was just too much to think about, and all of the time she could have spent thinking about it had been taken up by doublets and couplets and Capulets and corpses—which is exactly what she had wanted to spend the summer thinking about, and her ability to pay attention to what was in front of her had helped her become her Best Self.

She'd done the work. She'd gotten what she wanted. She'd visited Peg, who was doing fine. She'd met Velvet's grandbaby. She'd invited Portia to The Coffee Shop. She'd spent an entire night at Last Call with SuStan. Larkin had even made time for the long-overdue, difficult conversation with Jiro Takashi about behaving professionally, in the theater—in Sahil Malhotra's office, to ensure the message was received—and a different, no-less-difficult conversation with Isabella Willis.

The trouble was that whenever anyone got what they wanted, in the theater, they immediately began wanting something else—and what Larkin Day wanted, more than anything, was to spend the next hour with her best friends, to drive over to the campsite and see the closing matinee with Ed, to strike the set, and to go to the cast party.

———

"How did you and Elliott decide to do all of this?" Larkin asked Anni. The two of them were standing in front of the enormous kitchen sink, Anni washing and Larkin drying. "How did you know it was what you wanted?"

"We talked about the kind of house we wanted before we started house-hunting," Anni said, "and then we ignored all houses that were more than two increments away from our ideal house."

Larkin rephrased her question. "How did you and Elliott decide to buy a home together so quickly?" She placed a plate into the glass-front cupboards. "And don't say it was because your apartment was too small for him. Elliott could have rented an apartment of his own."

"Yes," Anni said. "That would have been the predictable thing to do." She passed another plate to Larkin. "Do you remember what I told you, when we were solving the Bonnie Cooper murder, about relationships?"

"Yes," Larkin said. "You shuffled a deck of cards and told me that when two people were willing to ask themselves what exists between them—"

"Or," Anni said, "what changes when they connect—"

"Then they have the possibility of creating something, together, that has never existed before." Larkin wiped the plate, remembering Anni's phrase. "In the known universe."

"Right," Anni said. "But that's where I got it wrong. It turns out that you have to shuffle more than once." She paused, turning off the faucet. "I didn't know this, otherwise I would have told you then. When you shuffle a deck of cards, just one time, there are still segments of predictability within the shuffle."

"Explain that like I'm a person who has never gone on a nerd cruise," Larkin said.

Anni thought, carefully, wringing the dripping dishrag over the empty sink. "So you've got a fresh deck of cards," she finally said, arranging the rag over the arch of the faucet. "It's in standard deck order, starting with the Ace of Hearts. You shuffle once. Some of those cards are in places you wouldn't be able to predict. Other cards are in places people can predict, especially people who do card tricks or people who count cards in casinos, because they know how the shuffling mechanic works."

"Okay," Larkin said.

"You have to shuffle seven times," Anni said, "before you get a deck that's considered random by our current mathematical standards."

"Okay," Larkin said again.

"Which means that when Elliott and I completed our first integration," Anni said, "there were many aspects of our relationship that were still fairly predictable. I would fuss about him leaving his stuff all over the place. He would fuss about me moving his stuff around. In a single-integration relationship, you get a tidy person and an untidy person. It's practically cliché."

"So you decided to buy a house together," Larkin said, "so Elliott would have more space for his stuff."

Anni shook her head. "We decided to buy a house together because we wanted to complete a second integration." She squirted some kind of lemon-and-lavender scented liquid onto a sponge and began wiping down the kitchen counter. "We could have wasted years going back and forth on *Anni is tidy and Elliott is untidy*. Blah, blah,

blah, why do you always leave your chessboards, blah, blah, blah, why do you care so much about which dish-towel I use."

"But you do care about the dishtowels," Larkin said. Anni had handed her, at the beginning of the dishwashing process, a very specific towel to use—along with instructions on how to use it.

"But talking about towels becomes much less important," Anni said, "when you have something more interesting to discuss. You figure out the towel thing, because it's no longer the big thing, and you can't do the big thing if you're still arguing about the towel thing." She scrubbed, a little harder, at a spot. "That's why we decided to do the big thing right away."

Larkin considered this. "But why did you pay cash? Why not do a mortgage?"

Anni wiped the freshly scrubbed spot with her thumb, satisfied that it had come clean. "We thought it was the best move," she said, "after we analyzed the potential variables." She turned to Larkin. Despite her handmade hair clips and her blue-and-white striped sundress, Anni looked older, somehow. It took work to change who you were, to reshuffle the cards and trust something you'd never tried before, to make the best moves whenever you could—and Anni, as usual, had done it all.

"Would you like me to tell you the variables?" she asked, squeezing out her sponge before placing it in a sponge-shaped dish. "I don't want to overwhelm you."

"I am in a beautiful old farmhouse that two of my best friends own outright," Larkin said, "after solving two murders and one attempted murder, saving the Summer Shakespeare Festival, burying my mother's girlfriend's dog, and signing up for an entire week of, like, hexagonal board games and twenty-sided dice." She filled the electric kettle and set it firmly on its base. Time for another cup of coffee. "So yes, please continue to overwhelm me."

"Well," Anni said, "the thing is that the value of money and the value of work are going to get really weird, really soon. Elliott and I have both built our careers on our ability to aggregate, organize, and transmit information to other people, for example. Now they're creating these internet-scrapers that can do all of that—you know, all of those chatbots and artbots they call *artificial intelligence*—and they're iterating them so quickly that they'll be able to make better choices than Elliott or I might have made, in terms of capturing attention."

She looked at Larkin, trusting her to understand. "Not that Elliott and I were ever in the attention-capturing business, of course. But these artificial intelligences are going to be very interested in eyes-on-screen, and they're going to transmit whatever information it takes to keep the eyes moving towards the ads."

Anni, in her kitchen, was calmer than Larkin had ever seen her. "You missed it, this summer. Search turned into shop. News turned into shop. Anything that could become a subscription did, including stuff you wouldn't expect, like, *cars*. You have to pay, monthly, for your seat heaters. Your friend Jay is making monthly payments to unlock his car's automatic high beams."

"He's not my friend," Larkin said. "I think he might be my nemesis."

"That's no good," Anni said. "We'll have to fix that." She made a note, in purple erasable marker, on the whiteboard that had been magnetized to their refrigerator. "There. I'll think about it later. Right now, I'm explaining to you why we paid cash for our home."

"Right," Larkin said. She had almost forgotten that was what this was about.

"Elliott thinks that there may be value in providing information to the AI, because right now they're just swallowing whatever they find online and regurgitating it in the aggregate, and there are going to be some copyright lawsuits coming, writers and artists are essentially waking up to discover that their life's work is being churned into chatbot chum, and even more importantly *they're not getting paid*, and there are two ways to get around this."

She held up one finger. "The first way is for the chatbots to subscribe to our content. If they want to create the world's best attention-grabbing chum, they have to pay each individual fish they swallow, every month."

"That's not going to happen," Larkin said.

"Of course not," Anni said. "Even though all of these bots know exactly whose content they grabbed, and how much of it they took. They have to, because of Fair Use laws—and if they aren't actually collecting that information, it'll come out in the lawsuits."

"So you and Elliott are both going to become lawyers," Larkin said.

"Absolutely not," Anni said. "Law is going to become a subscription, like healthcare and Jay's car. Lawyers are going to become programs, which is to say they're going to become chatbots. I suppose Elliott could write some of those programs, if he wanted to. But he's more interested in the way we're all going to manage information."

She held up her other finger. "That's the second way that people can make money in all of this *while still being people*. The bots are going to need high-quality information, once they are no longer allowed to scrape the internet like the bottom of a shoe. They'll need people who understand how things work. They'll need people who can distinguish false from true. They'll need *librarians*, for lack of a better word—and Elliott and I are preparing to pivot both of our careers in that direction."

"What happens if you don't make the pivot?"

"Well," Anni said, "we don't have a mortgage."

The electric kettle bubbled and then clicked; Larkin opened the cupboard that contained the coffee. She knew —she'd known since she walked in—that she could make herself at home here. So had Ed, who joined them in the kitchen to show them the latest photos on his phone.

"Portia and Farah," Larkin said. "Are those their moms?"

"Yes," Ed said. "Look how happy they are."

"Look how happy we are," Larkin said, wrapping her arms around Ed's waist and kissing him. The best thing she'd done that summer—the thing she couldn't tell anybody, not even Anni—was to stay out of the way of Ed and Portia's friendship. To let them be their Best Selves, without her, so she could be her Best Self with Ed, in her best friend's kitchen, on a beautiful Sunday afternoon.

"How could we not be happy?" Ed asked. "We're going on a nerd cruise!"

"I know!" Larkin said. She called out, loud enough for Elliott and Josephine and Claire to hear. "We're going on a nerd cruise!"

"Larkin!" her mother called back. "Why are you shouting? Is everything okay in there?"

"Yes," Larkin said, turning towards the parlor door, looking at all of the people who loved her. "Everything's cool."

Larkin may think she's going on vacation—but that's before she finds a murder to solve and a manuscript to recover. Join Larkin, Ed, Anni, Elliott, Josephine, Claire and all the other nerds as they experience a week of gaming, magic, math, and music—plus formal dinners, foam weaponry, and a body that is missing its head. MURDER ON THE NERD CRUISE is coming in 2024.

BONUS STORY
"ALL I WANT FOR CHRISTMAS IS MURDER"

This piece originally ran in Shortwave Magazine on December 7, 2022.

The events take place between *Ode to Murder* and *Like, Subscribe, and Murder*, although you don't need to have read either book to enjoy the story.

(We do suggest you read both books.)

(And everything else Shortwave publishes.)

"ALL I WANT FOR CHRISTMAS IS MURDER"
A LARKIN DAY HOLIDAY SHORT

"The truth," Ben sang, his baritone quavering against the eighth notes. "I only want the truth, it's all I want from you, it's true, it's doable if you are fully present, it's pleasant, it's—"

Larkin set down her glass of spiced wine. She wrote *Is truth pleasant?* on a yellow legal pad. Ben, at the end of both his breath and his tether, watched her.

"Is something wrong?" he asked. "I know it's pitchy."

"It's off-pitchy," Ed said, from his seat at the piano. "Pun intended."

"Drink," Ben said, picking up his glass of water. He was forgoing wine, wassail, and nog until the rehearsal, workshop, or whatever-it-was when Ed and Larkin met with Ben and Mitchell to go over the newest pages of Ben's opera-in-progress, was over.

Larkin sipped her wine, which tasted of ginger and cloves. Mitchell, from his seat by the fireplace, raised a tiny crystal glass of single-malt scotch. Ed, whose intent towards wordplay had prompted Ben to invent the drinking game, had tea. The four of them—Ed, wearing a

Fair Isle sweater that matched the violet in his Black skin; Larkin, wearing a worn-out hoodie that was the same color as her long, dark hair; Ben, wearing floppy plaid slippers and a thermal shirt with *Naughty* printed on the front in red sequins; Mitchell, who had zipped the majority of the *Nice* shirt behind a sleek fleece pullover—had been working together for a little over a month. Their games had gotten better. Ben's opera hadn't.

"What do you think, love?" Ben directed this question towards Mitchell—who deflected, as he always did, with "I think you're doing very well."

"So why am I off pitch?" Ben asked. Larkin could have answered him; her legal pad was already filled with notes like *where is the melody* and *I have never heard these intervals before* and *I'm not sure anyone has*. But whenever any of them hinted to Ben that his opera might lack a certain musicality, he reminded them that he wasn't writing a musical.

So Larkin and Ed sat, silently, sending glances to each other like flares, until Ben said "This is a real question, not a rhetorical one."

"It could be that you just haven't learned it yet," said Mitchell, from his corner. He was halfway through his scotch, and this was the closest he'd get to giving Ben any actual criticism. The two of them were about to celebrate their fifth anniversary.

"How could I not have *learned* it?" This time Ben's question was a retort. "I *wrote* it."

Larkin and Ed were about to celebrate five weeks of dating, give or take—and Ed, after another rapid passing of glances, took the responsibility of responding. "The human voice," he said, "the human *brain*, really, works on a system of heuristics. We fill in the patterns we expect to find. When I hear you sing this melodic line, I hear your voice automatically working to create consonant intervals instead of some of the dissonances you've written."

"It's not a melodic line," Ben said. "That is the whole point. The dissonances are written *with intent*."

"I know," Ed said, carefully, "but—"

He looked at Larkin. She looked at her legal pad. Then she looked at Ben and told him the unpleasant truth.

"It sounds like your brain is trying to rewrite the music," Larkin said. "Maybe towards what it should be."

"There is no *should* in creativity," Ben said. "Sondheim didn't *should*."

Larkin looked towards Mitchell, who raised his glass. The two of them had joked, after one of the previous rehearsals, whether they should drink not only every time Ed made a pun, but also every time Ben referenced Stephen Sondheim. They hadn't mentioned this to Ben, of course. Larkin hadn't even told Ed, but she saw him sip carefully from his mug of peppermint tea and suspected he had figured it out on his own.

"Why don't we take a break?" Mitchell asked. He took the stage manager role, when the four of them gathered in Ben and Mitchell's mansion to listen to Ben sing his way through the opera. Sometimes Ed sang, when the part called for a tenor. Larkin had tried singing alto, the first time they gathered—and after commenting that she had never seen so many notes packed into a single measure, was quickly promoted to director.

Which was fine by her. She liked directing. Larkin had always been good at helping people solve problems. It was one of the reasons why she had decided to become a private detective. The other reason, of course, was that detective work paid better. Only the best theater directors were able to earn more than the average private detective, after all—and Larkin was pretty sure she could do at least an average job of solving mysteries.

———

"I mean," Larkin told Mitchell, the two of them standing on either side of a granite-topped kitchen island, "I'd like to be the best private detective in Pratincola, Iowa someday."

"Good for you," Mitchell said, slicing a wedge off the kind of cheese that had a rind on the outside and veins on the inside. He offered the wedge to Larkin, along with a fresh glass of fragrant wine from the copper kettle kept simmering on the stove. "Because there's something I need you to solve."

"A murder?" Larkin might not have responded so impulsively if she had eaten the cheese before sipping the wine—her third glass, but that was only because Ben had mentioned Sondheim five times that afternoon.

Mitchell slid a sleeve of water crackers onto the cutting board next to the cheese. Then he opened a container of imported dates. "No," he said, taking out a two-pronged fork that was slightly bigger than his index finger. Larkin would have used a regular fork, or maybe one of those toothpicks with the bit of plastic on the end if it were a special occasion. "Just a mystery."

"Okay," Larkin said, trying not to sound disappointed. "Probably better for everyone that way. Fewer dead bodies." She really shouldn't drink any more wine until she ate at least two more wedges of cheese.

"No bodies, *per se*," Mitchell said, "but Ben has informed me that he has already given me plenty of clues about what he wants for Christmas." He passed Larkin a fork-pronged date. "And if I don't figure it out, our relationship is *effectively dead.*"

He said the last part in Ben's voice, or at least Ben's inflections—Mitchell would have made a decent actor, if he hadn't decided to make an indecent amount of money in Cedar Rapids business development—and Larkin accepted both the appetizer and the assignment. "All right," she said, "so what were the clues?"

Mitchell sighed. He was older than Ben, passing off his former hairline as a high forehead, smoothing his worn knuckles with what Larkin assumed was a very expensive hand cream. "If I had any idea what the clues were, I might be able to solve the mystery myself."

"So that's why you're hiring me," Larkin said.

The corner of Mitchell's mouth quirked, turning him from *older man* to *silver fox*. "I'm asking you," he said. "As a friend."

Larkin, who had lived in Pratincola for just over four months, needed friends as much as she needed money. "All right," she said, raising her glass of Christmas-flavored wine. "Larkin Day is on the case."

The lights flickered. "Is your house, like, programmed to do that?" Ben and Mitchell's home did a lot of things, many of which continued to surprise her. The floors were heated, for example. So were the toilets.

"No," Mitchell said. "I was expecting weather, but not until later this evening." Then he said—not to Larkin, but to the kitchen in general—"Immediate forecast."

"The next hour is likely to include freezing rain with winds as high as 29 miles per hour." his kitchen responded, in a voice that suggested that one of his appliances had trained at the Royal Shakespeare Company. "Stay indoors. Large, dangerous hailstones may make driving difficult."

The lights flickered again. "You've gotten used to Iowa weather, I assume?" Mitchell asked.

Larkin hadn't—but if she was going to be a Pratincolan, she needed to start acting like one. "It's just another storm," she said. "It's not like we're going to be stuck in your gigantic mansion in the middle of nowhere with no power and no phones and, like, *the bridge going out*."

"The bridge won't go out," Mitchell said. "But it freezes before the road does."

———

"Ben says we might need to spend the night," Ed said, when Larkin returned to the music room. He looked like he liked the idea. Larkin couldn't tell if it was because Ed was looking forward to spending the night with her, or whether he was looking forward to spending the night in a house with heated floors and talking appliances and a canister-shaped device that could travel from room to room at will. They could call the robot, if that was the appropriate thing to call it, and it would orient itself towards the sound of their voices. Then it would beep and chirp and bring them snacks.

It could bring them anything, really. Just because Ben and Mitchell had filled its head with chocolate squares and pretzel sticks didn't mean there wasn't room to cram anything else into its interior. If Larkin were going to leave clues for someone to find, she would start there.

"Artie," she called out. A confident chirp came from another part of the house, and Larkin responded to the unspoken question. "Music room."

"How does it hear you?" Ed asked. "Is the entire house wired? What does that even mean? I feel like I just said that because I heard it in a movie somewhere."

"This whole house is like a movie," Larkin said. "A mysterious mansion, a threatening storm, a series of clues that have to be uncovered before someone gets murdered."

"The only thing getting murdered in this mansion is *tonality*," Ed quipped, as the snack canister rolled its way into the room. Larkin watched its sensor flick first towards Ed, then towards her.

"It's me, Artie," she said. "I want to see if Ben put anything in your head."

"Why would I put anything in Artie's head?" It was Ben, back in the room, with his enormous water bottle and his even more enormous opera score.

Larkin pressed the button that opened Artie's cranium. "Because Mitchell says you've been leaving him clues." There was nothing inside Artie except the kind of snacks that were only sold at grocery stores named after fictional explorers.

"Clues?"

"About what you want for Christmas."

"Oh," Ben said, smiling with understanding. "Right." He reached into Artie and pulled out a single piece of black licorice. "And did Mitchell ask you to figure out what those clues were?"

"Yes," Larkin said, smiling right back.

"You know," Ed said, "you could just tell him what you wanted—"

"No, no, no!" Ben said, popping the licorice into his mouth and sucking the residue off his fingers. "Then it wouldn't be any *fun*. Not when I know my husband is so *clueless*—"

He paused, glancing meaningfully at Ed.

"Pun intended?" Ed asked.

Ben uncorked his water bottle. "Well, we know somebody's paying attention," he said, as he and Larkin drank. "Not Mitchell, though. He had to hire a detective."

"I'm not getting paid," Larkin said. "Mitchell was very clear about that."

"It may be the only thing he's been *clear about* all afternoon," Ben said, and this time his voice flickered along with the lights. Something was troubling him. Something true. Something unpleasant. Something dark, and—Larkin saw it in Ben's face, right before the lights went out—*effectively deadly.*

———

"You should ask him," Larkin said, keeping her voice light, as she and Ed sat together on the piano bench while Mitchell and Ben rustled up flashlights and candles. The house had emergency bulbs built in, of course, safely illuminating the walls and corners. Their phones had flashlights built in as well, if it came to it—but Mitchell was a Boomer and Ben was a romantic, and so they had each gone off in search of their preferred lighting source. Larkin and Ed had remained, Larkin scooching close enough to Ed for their arms to brush against each other every time one of them breathed.

"Ask him what?"

"What the clues were." Larkin took a cookie-butter-flavored cookie out of Artie's head, which could not close until both the power and the Wi-Fi came back on. Mitchell had suggested they eat anything inside Artie that might spoil. Ben had reminded Mitchell that they could always transfer everything from Artie's head to the kitchen refrigerator, which had backup power. Mitchell had reminded Ben that they would have to carry each individual item by hand, since Artie's wheels were no longer functional.

Larkin had watched the two of them argue with each other, and wondered how much of it played into the game they were playing. She wondered how much of the game was serious, and whether Ben's game was more serious than any of them suspected.

"You think he'll tell me?" Ed, who was better about following directions than Larkin was, had selected the sliced prosciutto.

"He likes you," Larkin said. "Everybody likes you."

This was true. It had become even more true in the past two months, after Larkin had solved a murder and Ed had saved the day. Now Larkin was hoping Ed could help her save this one—and, if the two of them got lucky, they could spend the night sleeping side-by-side in one of Ben and Mitchell's guest bedrooms.

Not that her relationship with Ed was purely physical, of course. It had barely been physical, up to that point. They had kissed, like, *once*. Twice, if Larkin counted the kiss she had given Ed right after she had turned a murderer—her *first* murderer—into police custody. But Larkin never counted that kiss. It had been spontaneous. For a kiss to mean anything, it had to be planned in advance.

So Larkin stared soulfully into Ed's eyes—the first step in the plan, after the preliminary steps of unzipping her hoodie and unponytailing her hair—until Ed started laughing. "Fine," he said. "I'll do it."

———

Ed wasn't able to get to his part of the plan until they had gotten through another hour of opera workshop. Ben sang so fervently that the candles went out; Larkin finished off the entire package of cookies. Mitchell sat in his leather armchair, interspersing continuous comments on how good Ben's opera was (it wasn't) with occasional glances at the window to see if it was still hailing (it was).

"You're going to have to stay here until morning, I'm afraid," he said.

Larkin was in no way afraid of this. She gave Ed her most seductive smile, fluttering her eyelashes flirtatiously and lowering the zipper on her hoodie another few inches. Ed laughed, again. She liked it when he laughed—the way it relaxed his face while simultaneously crinkling it up—but it didn't seem like the kind of step that would lead towards the kind of kiss she wanted. Maybe they'd get to that after Ed got the clues out of Ben.

But Ed reported, after the rehearsal had ended and he had followed Ben into the basement to get more candles, that Ben was unwilling to cooperate. "I'm on to you, Ed Jackson," Ben had said, the two of them using one of Mitchell's flashlights to navigate the darkness. "You're just trying to get me to tell you what I told Mitchell so you can tell Larkin."

"Which means we don't have any new clues," Ed said, tilting his head close enough to Larkin's for them to speak *sotto voce*.

"Yes, we do," Larkin whispered back. "We know that the clues weren't written down. Ben told them to Mitchell."

"So we can stop looking inside robot heads," Ed said, his voice tickling the inside of Larkin's ear.

"Yes," Larkin said. "But we might want to ask the robots a few questions."

———

The first question was directed towards Mitchell. "Does your house, like, record everything?"

"What do you mean?" Mitchell was chopping scallions. Larkin was helping, in the sense that she had taken a scallion out of its produce bag and handed it to Mitchell. The rest of her senses had been handed over to the mystery.

"I mean," Larkin said, "your kitchen knows when you ask it for a weather update. That must mean it keeps track of what you say."

"Ah," Mitchell said, scooping up the scallions and scattering them over a hot skillet. He had lit the gas stove with a long wooden match, and was now using it to prepare supper. "Yes, our conversation is being recorded," he said, mixing the scallions into the garlic-butter mixture that had just started to brown, "or it would be, if the Wi-Fi was currently working."

"So we could access those recordings somewhere," Larkin said, "and find the clues Ben gave you."

Mitchell turned down the burner and turned his attention towards the palm-sized slabs of beef that Larkin already knew must have cost more than her shoes. "Not necessarily. Smart home devices may record everything, but that's only so they can process the data for key commands."

"Like the weather command," Larkin said.

"Exactly," Mitchell said. He put the beef on the skillet with his bare hands. Then he washed his hands carefully, with soap. "Any data that does not contain a key command gets discarded."

"Which means the data with key commands gets saved," Larkin said. She handed Mitchell a dishtowel. "Why?"

"So they can analyze it," Mitchell said. "How quickly the command was observed, how long it took for the device to respond, how the device handles the same commands spoken by different voices. Whether the device responds to an item that isn't a key command, or whether the device misses a command."

"How would the device know if it missed a command?"

"You say *missed command*," Mitchell said, as if that explained everything. "Then it checks what was just recorded for what might have been missed."

"Aha!" Larkin said, just like a real detective. "Then it does keep the old recordings!"

"Not *forever*," Mitchell said.

"Nothing is *forever*," Ben said, entering the kitchen as if he had been waiting for an opening. "Recordings get erased. Relationships end. People lie and then they *die*." He picked up the two-pronged fork and stabbed it into a piece of simmering garlic.

"Ben," Mitchell said, "that's hot."

"I don't care," Ben said. "I'll burn my mouth. It's not like I'm going to be using it to kiss you any time soon." He turned to Larkin. "Did you know that my husband asked a detective to figure out what I asked him to get me for Christmas?" He waved the fork around, circling dangerously close to Mitchell's cheek and Larkin's décolletage, before stabbing it into the cutting board. "Oh, wait, you did! Because *you're the detective*."

He stalked off. Larkin zipped her hoodie all the way up to her neck.

"Well," Mitchell said, "someone's in a mood."

"It's the holidays," Larkin said, even though she was pretty sure it wasn't. "Everybody gets stressed out around the holidays."

"I just wish I knew what he wanted me to get him, so I could go buy it and we could stop arguing over it,"

Mitchell said. "Last year he wanted that snack robot, and even though we already had a mini-bar in the lounge and a mini-fridge in the billiard room I went ahead and bought it for him."

"You have a billiard room?"

"Of course." Mitchell pressed the flat of his thumb carefully against the top of each beef medallion."I mean, it's really a game room." He flipped them over and began drizzling butter-garlic-scallion sauce over the cooked sides. "With a pool table."

"And it's not, like, connected to the lounge by a secret passage or anything, right?"

"Of course not," Mitchell said. "Any self-respecting engineer puts his secret passage in the library."

———

The next step was, of course, to meet Ed in the secret passage. This step had to wait until after supper, during which Ben sloshed his way through all of the alcohol he had refused to consume all afternoon—Larkin wondered why Mitchell appeared unconcerned, until she realized that Ben was much more interested in using his glass to gesture dramatically than he was in *drinking from it*—and Ed tried to save the day with questions and quips. The power came back on shortly after they sat down, increasing the electricity between the husbands. Ben, shooting sparks; Mitchell, fraying.

"I wish you'd just tell me what I've done wrong," Mitchell finally said, when he stood to clear their plates. It wasn't meant for Larkin and Ed to hear, so they tried not to look as if they were trying to listen.

"That's the problem," Ben said. "You don't even know *what it is*."

He sat, one slippered foot on the edge of the burgundy-and-gold upholstered chair, and took out his phone. "I'm going to check my messages," he said, as Ed and Larkin helped Mitchell with the dishes.

"You don't need to do that," Mitchell said, as Ed looked for a place to put his empty water glass. "The two of you are our guests, although I'm afraid we're not being very good hosts. Is there anything I can do to distract you from what you just saw?"

Larkin asked herself *what Mitchell wanted*. She couldn't give him the solution to his mystery, but she could give him the opportunity to show off. "We want to see the secret passage," she said.

"All right," Mitchell said. "I'll take you to the library."

———

The secret passage, as Mitchell explained, was meant to be found. It was a bookcase door that Larkin opened by pulling on a faux book titled *The History of Secret Passages*.

"There it is," Mitchell said, ushering them both inside. "Feel free to look around. The exit door leads to the lounge, but you won't be able to open it because it's currently blocked by a Christmas tree."

He closed the entrance door behind him, leaving Larkin and Ed bookended by darkness.

"I feel like we should be helping with the dishes," Ed said—whispered, really, even though the passage wasn't secret enough for them to need to be quiet. "Mitchell has been feeding us all day."

"Yeah, I know," Larkin whispered back. Her plan to spend a romantic night with Ed had not accounted for cookies and dates and cheese and wine and olives and grapes and nuts and the best steak she had ever eaten and steamed asparagus and pan-fried sweet potatoes and a slice of fruitcake soaked in brandy and a tiny cup of espresso. She wasn't sure whether she wanted Ed to see her with her pants off, at this point—but she wasn't sure how much longer she could keep her pants on. "We'll help by solving the mystery," she said, to take her mind off the unpleasant truth of how much she had eaten.

They walked slowly down the passage. It was hard to tell where they were going; Larkin tried to move the mansion around in her head so she could get a sense of where they were. Then they stopped—Larkin placing a warning hand on Ed's shoulder—because they could hear Ben's voice.

"Yeah," Ben said. "Yeah. He says I'm being a baby."

"We must be outside the dining room," Larkin whispered.

"He didn't really say that." This was a different voice, coming out of Ben's phone's speaker.

"That's Shawnta," Ed whispered. Shawnta, who worked at the Cedar Rapids Public Library and sang occasional solos with the Pratincola Concert Choir, was one of Ben's best friends.

"Well, he *as good as said it*," Ben said. "You know how he looks, sometimes. Like I'm the youngest, neediest man in the world."

"Does the shoe fit?"

"I'm not wearing shoes," Ben said. "Only these old worn-out slippers. I want Mitchell to get me a pair of those heated slippers, you know, the kind that you plug into the wall every night, for Christmas."

Larkin looked at Ed. "Is that it?" she whispered. "Heated slippers?"

"Of course," Ben continued, "I can't ask him for heated slippers until he figures out what I really want."

"What do you really want?" Shawnta asked.

Ben laughed. It was not a nice laugh. "I can't tell *you!* The walls have ears."

"Right," Shawnta said. "Your entire house is, like, wired for eavesdropping."

"Plus," Ben continued, "Mitchell has Larkin on detective duty, like he thinks I'm going to murder him if he doesn't get it right or something."

"Are you?"

"Like I'd ever say that out loud."

That gave Larkin an idea.

"Do you have your phone?" she whispered, to Ed. "Can you text Shawnta?"

She would have done it herself, except Shawnta wasn't one of her contacts. Instead, she dictated:

Larkin and I are in Ben and Mitchell's secret passage.

Please ask Ben to text you what he wants Mitchell to give him for Christmas.

Ed had added the *please.*

Then please let us know what he tells you.

She watched Ed as he sent one more text:

It's no fun watching Ben and Mitchell fight. Trust me.

She waited. Then she heard Ben's phone chime with a new notification.

"Ooh," Ben said. "Shawnta, you delicious maven of information management. Sure, I'll text you."

They waited, again. Then Ed's phone lit up—and chimed twice.

He's going to do it

Hold for more info

"Excuse me," Ben said. They heard him stand up. "Is someone *texting* in the secret passage?"

"Why is your phone set to *sound*?" Larkin whispered.

"Why wouldn't it be?" Ed whispered back.

Larkin, whose phone was nearly always set to *silent*, hadn't considered what might happen if Ben realized that Shawnta was acting on their behalf—but it happened very, very quickly.

"Did Ed and Larkin ask you to solve their mystery for them?" Ben said, loud enough for both the secret passage and the speakerphone. He was moving, his slippered feet slapping against the dining room floor, his voice carrying throughout the house.

"I'm sorry," Shawnta said, her voice crackling as Ben traveled. "Ed said he hated seeing you and Mitchell fight."

"We're not fighting," Ben said. "We are deciding, once and for all, whether we love each other." That was loud enough for Mitchell to hear it, in the kitchen.

"Mitchell loves you!" Ed called out, from the passage.

"You know that!" Larkin echoed. It seemed like the right thing to say, even though she wasn't at all sure whether it was true. How would Ben know if Mitchell loved him? Why did he think Mitchell didn't? What had happened between the two of them, and how had she missed it?

"You two are *not helping*," Ben said. He was in the library, now, his voice a few feet away. There was a thump. A grunt. The sound of something being dragged across the hardwood. "Pun intended, as Dr. Ed Jackson might say."

"What was the pun?" Ed whispered.

"Now I'm going to have a drink," Ben said—and then both his footsteps and his voice disappeared.

Larkin turned on her flashlight and made her way to the bookcase door. There was a hand-sized hole that allowed her to push the faux book out of place, triggering the latch that opened the door—but the door itself was blocked by an enormous wing-backed chair. That was what Ben had thumped and grunted and dragged across the floor.

For a minute, Larkin was relieved. She didn't really think Ben had murdered Mitchell; she'd never really thought Ben would. But she hadn't expected Ben to shut them inside the secret passage. Of course, she hadn't expected there to *be* a secret passage—or an impenetrable storm, or an impassable bridge, or an insoluble mystery.

"Are you going to leave us in here forever?" Larkin shouted, through the hole in the door. "We're just trying to help!"

There was a flash of light, somewhere in the library; an imperceptible electronic chirp.

"Oh wait," Ed said, "I get it. That's the pun. He's going to keep us from helping."

"Not when Larkin Day is on the case," Larkin said.

The light flashed, again. The chirp chirped.

"What is that?" Larkin pushed her cheek as close to the door hole as possible until she caught it in her peripheral vision. Artie, the snack robot, in some kind of docking station.

"Why is Artie chirping?" Larkin asked. This time Artie chirped more confidently, swiveling its robot eyes towards the secret door. She turned to Ed. "Do you think we can get it to push the chair out of the way?"

"I don't know," Ed said. "It sounded like the chair was so heavy that Ben could barely move it."

"I don't want to break their robot," Larkin said. She tilted her face again, to see as much of Artie as possible. "Are you capable of pushing a chair?"

The flash. The chirp. Maybe Artie was.

"Artie!" Larkin said. "Secret passage!"

The robot undocked itself. It rolled carefully towards

the secret passage door. Then it stopped, flashed its little red light over the wing-back chair, and beeped sadly.

"It's okay," Larkin said. "You're still our favorite robot."

Flash. Chirp.

"Our tea," Ed said, each word loud and distinct.

Artie made the confident chirp. Its eyes swiveled towards the door.

"Don't say anything," Ed whispered. "Tell me when it's eyes close."

Larkin watched. "Okay," she whispered. "I think it's gone back to sleep."

"Our slippers," Ed said, as before.

Artie made the quiet chirp. Its lights flickered but did not open into eyes.

"Artie."

Confident chirp.

"Are you listening?"

Quiet chirp.

"I think it's programmed to activate whenever it hears the *R* sound," Ed said.

"No," Larkin said, remembering her conversation with Mitchell. "It's programmed to *save the recording*."

———

Are you free
  i could be

The reply was from Larkin's best friend Anni, whose texts never contained capital letters even though it took extra work to decapitalize them. It was a necessary distinction, Anni had explained. It separated texting from other forms of communication.

At that moment, Larkin was only interested in forms of

communication that might have been stored within a canister-shaped recording device.

This is for a mystery, Larkin texted.

a murder mystery

It could be, Larkin texted. Then she added the winking emoji. *Probably just a regular mystery tho*

Larkin and Anni had agreed, when they first became friends, that they were allowed to make jokes about the mysteries Larkin solved. Especially the ones that involved murder. It was a necessary release, Anni had explained. Something to do with the heart rate tracker she wore on her wrist and all of the other metrics she continually managed.

I am in a secret passage with Ed. Larkin added the heart-eyes emoji.

Can you look up the instruction manual for the SmartHome Friend

And tell me how to access its stored recordings?

Artie's brand name was printed across the bottom of its docking station. Larkin could have downloaded its instruction manual herself, but she didn't have time to read a 150-page PDF on her phone. Anni would be able to scan the text and pull out the relevant details faster than—

larkin it is very easy

say "play stored recordings"

"Play stored recordings," Larkin said.

Artie did not respond.

it erases its stored recordings every day at midnight

"Play stored recordings," Larkin said again.

and it only records for five seconds after it hears its wake word

"Artie," Larkin said. "Play stored recordings."

Artie chirped.

Its eyes began to glow.

"Artie," the robot said, in Ben's voice. "Bedroom."

"Are you going to be there?" Ben's voice, again.

"Our friends." That was Mitchell. "And anyway—"

Ben: "Aren't going to be helpful then—"

Mitchell: "Art is hard. I can see you're working—"

Ben: "Harder when you don't—"

Mitchell: "Aren't happy with it then keep working—"

Ben: "Our marriage is based on truth."

Ben, again: "Are you going to be honest with me?"

Larkin turned to Ed. "I think I know what Ben wants."

"Good," Ed said, "because I just texted Mitchell to get us out of here."

———

Artie continued to play its stored recordings as Mitchell and Ben worked together to carry the chair back to where it belonged. None of them were as revealing as what Larkin and Ed had already heard, but it didn't matter—the answer had already been revealed, and all Larkin had to do was present her solution.

"Sit down, all of you," she said. Mitchell took the wing-back. Ben took the overstuffed armchair. Ed looked around for a third chair, and ended up sitting on the middle step of the library ladder.

Larkin began pacing. It seemed like the kind of thing a detective would do, in a not-quite-manor-house, not-quite-murder-mystery. "What does Ben want for Christmas?" She paused, every few steps, to stare at whichever man was closest. Ed stifled a laugh. Ben narrowed his eyes. Mitchell stared back, and Larkin held her gaze until he finally blinked.

"If you asked Ben to circle an item in a catalog," Larkin said, remembering too late that people no longer did that, "he would pick a pair of heated slippers that you can plug into the wall."

"We have heated floors," Mitchell said.

"Not when the power goes out," Ben sniped.

"Be quiet, both of you," Larkin said. She paced another few rounds, stopping at intervals to stare. Ben stuck his tongue out. Ed blushed. Mitchell didn't blink.

"What does Ben *really* want?" she asked.

The trouble was that she couldn't remember the intervals, not even after hearing Ben fail to sing them earlier that afternoon. His opera wasn't working—and Ben knew it, and Ed knew it, and Larkin knew it, and Mitchell knew it.

But Mitchell was the only one who wasn't saying it.

So Larkin sang.

"The truth, he only wants the truth, it's all Ben wants from you, it's true, it's doable, he wants it for his present, even if it's unpleasant—"

"It's all I've ever asked for," Ben continued, picking up the aria where Larkin had misplaced it, "and if I take you to task, it's only that I'm lonely for the man who used to only speak the truth."

Mitchell applauded. Then he sighed. "Your opera is terrible."

"I know."

"I didn't tell you because I thought it would discourage you from figuring out how to make it better."

"What you did was even more discouraging," Ben said. "I felt like you weren't taking me seriously."

"I take everything you do seriously," Mitchell said. "Why do you think I asked a detective to help me figure out what I had missed?"

"Why didn't you ask me?"

"Because—" Larkin watched Mitchell decide to tell the

truth. "You say things without saying them, and you assume I understand them, and when I don't, you give me that look."

"What look?"

"Like I'm the oldest, neediest man in the world."

The two men looked at each other, an entire story shifting between their eyes.

"Well," Ben said, "I don't mind needing you if you don't mind needing me."

Mitchell reached out a hand towards Ben, who reached back. "I've never minded."

They connected.

————

"You know," Ed said, as he and Larkin were unwrapping fresh toothbrushes in Ben and Mitchell's guest bathroom, "you got it right from the very beginning."

"What do you mean?"

"The answer was in Artie's head all along," Ed said, smiling. "The robot butler."

"It's always the butler," Larkin said.

"No," Ed said. "It's always Larkin."

Then he kissed her. Larkin didn't know if he'd planned to—it didn't seem like sinks and toothpaste would have been part of his plan—but it didn't matter anymore. She'd gotten what she wanted. They all had.

ACKNOWLEDGMENTS

Thanks, as always, to Alan and Larry and my parents.
Thanks, for the first time, to Beth and Jim.
Thanks, in perpetuity, to you.

ABOUT THE AUTHOR

Nicole Dieker is a writer, teacher, and musician. She began her writing career as a full-time freelancer with a focus on personal finance and habit formation; she launched her fiction career with *The Biographies of Ordinary People*, a definitely-not-autobiographical novel that follows three sisters from 1989 to 2016.

Currently, Dieker writes the *Larkin Day* mystery series and the perzine *WHAT IT IS and WHAT TO DO NEXT*. She also maintains an active freelance career; her work has appeared in Vox, Morning Brew, Lifehacker, Bankrate, Haven Life, Popular Science, and more. Dieker spent five years as writer and editor for The Billfold, a personal finance blog where people had honest conversations about money.

Praise from Kirkus Reviews: "Dieker excels at depicting how real people think and act."

Dieker lives in Quincy, Illinois with the great love of her life, his piano, and their garden.

A NOTE FROM SHORTWAVE PUBLISHING

Thank you for reading Larkin's third mystery! If you enjoyed *Shakespeare in the Park with Murder*, please consider writing a review. Reviews help readers find more titles they may enjoy, and that helps us continue to publish titles like this.

For more Shortwave fiction, free-to-read Magazine stories, newsletters, author events, limited editions, and more, please visit us online…

OUR WEBSITE

shortwavepublishing.com

on TWITTER and INSTAGRAM

@ShortwaveBooks

EMAIL US

contact@shortwavepublishing.com

www.ingramcontent.com/pod-product-compliance
Lightning Source LLC
Chambersburg PA
CBHW021312190726
48288CB00003B/808